KRISTA SCHADE

BY KRISTA SCHADE

The Clothesline Series:
The Clothesline
Lone Wolfe

Biographies:
A Living History – Uncle Col Walker

For Children:
T-Bone and the Mob, with Lisa Brettschneider

www.kristaschade.com.au

LONE WOLFE

By Krista Schade

LONE WOLFE

This book is a work of fiction.
Names, characters, and places are the product of the author's imagination or are used fictitiously.
Any resemblance to actual locales or persons, living or dead, is coincidental.

First published in 2021

A catalogue record for this book is available from the National Library of Australia

ISBN **978-0-6489020-5-8**

CHAPTER 1 - LACHLAN

Lachlan Wolfe watched the naked figure cross the room in front of him, her feet caressed by the deep carpet that muffled her graceful movements. The woman was beautiful, her body lean and tanned, and the hair that cascaded down her bare back was dark and luxurious. The early morning light streaming through the penthouse windows illuminated her beauty in the most sensual way, however Lachlan was unmoved. She was exactly his type - confident, unashamed, and poised - yet he felt no stirring, either beneath the sheet, or within his heart.

The night was now a bit of a blur - a charity gala, a bevy of gorgeous women, then locked in the lift with this raven beauty, each passionately clawing at the other as the lift whizzed them to his apartment.

Just another Saturday night for Lachlan. He was unabashedly certain in his ability to attract people to him, like dull moths to a dazzling flame. So many women, and often men, wanted a piece of the Lone Wolfe, as he was affectionately known in the press, and most wanted to tame him in matrimony. His name, combined with his charm and haunting good looks, proved over and over to be an intoxicating combination.

She turned and caught his gaze, and from her slow smile Lachlan knew she had misunderstood his scrutiny.

"Good morning, Senator." Her voice was low purr and no doubt sexy as hell, yet he was keen to extract himself and ensure there was no awkward misunderstanding.

His head felt achy, and his mouth was dry, thanks to last night's copious amounts of red wine, and he struggled to remember her name.

Ashley? Courtney? Trinity? He really had no idea. He should feel bad about that, he supposed, but as usual he just felt empty.

He sat up a little in the wide bed, his broad chest bare. He was careful to keep the crisp sheets covering his disinterested lower half, and he arranged his handsome features into what he hoped was an expression of kindness.

"I'm so sorry," he began. "I really have a full schedule today, and I am sure you have...." What was it she said she did again? Something corporate, perhaps law. He took a guess. "... a case to continue on with, so perhaps we can arrange something for next week?" He noted the disappointment as it began to cloud her pretty face, but he ploughed on. The morning after platitudes seemed to almost speak for themselves nowadays.

"I will organise a driver for you now, so I am not keeping you any longer."

He allowed his voice to drop slightly and injected some suggestiveness - he did not want to burn bridges entirely.

"But I do appreciate the time you have given me already." He hoped his hair would be sexily tousled and not a downright mess.

The woman in front of him was not convinced. He could tell by the way she quickly dressed that she was not buying his banter, and when she tossed him her card before she marched out the door of the main suite, he realised his error.

'Cassidy Marlow - Social Influencer'

Ouch - so not a lawyer then. He had the good grace to wince slightly, remembering that the feisty, busty barrister he had confused her with was a conquest from a few days ago.

Oh well. He doubted they would cross paths again, and if they did, she could decide whether to try again or ignore him; either way he was not concerned.

He slid back down into the large bed, closed his eyes, and allowed sleep to reclaim him.

A few hours later Lachlan had showered, shaved, and hit the gym for a punishing workout, ruthlessly squeezing the last of the previous night's excesses from his body. Back in the penthouse he threw together a thick protein shake and showered again, before heading downstairs to his waiting car.

The traffic was not heavy, and Lachlan's mood lifted as he joined the modest stream of cars flowing along the city streets. Society was easing back into normality now that lockdown restrictions had eased.

International travel was still grounded, and Lachlan wondered if he would ever feel comfortable shut into an aeroplane with hundreds of strangers, all breathing the same air in and out, in and out. The pandemic has changed so many things about the world as he knew it, but he also felt changed; he had seen too much.

As a newly elected Senator he had enjoyed not quite 12 months of hard political jostling before the virus emerged and not long after the first anniversary of his successful electoral campaign, he found himself living at the House, a virtual prisoner of the people.

He understood the need for caution - then and now - but living and working in the House, had been difficult.

He remembered with a sense of shame how alone and isolated he had felt; weakness in any form was not appealing. When he allowed it, survivor guilt clenched his stomach too; his family had emerged unscathed, cocooned by wealth and privilege.

Apart from faithfully serving his constituents, who had needed him then more than ever, there had only been one spark of happiness during that time, but that fruitless, reckless romance had survived mere months. Rightly so, he reminded himself, deliberately steering his thoughts away from Kate. Kate who had returned to her husband and left his heart aching.

He swung the sleek sedan into the paved driveway of his parents northside estate and deftly keyed the security code into the panel, awakening the heavy ornate metal gates. They parted gracefully and he drove along the tree lined avenue to the front of the house.

The day was warm and as he stepped from the car Lachlan spied his mother in the garden, gesturing with the gardener, who respectfully nodded along as she explained some grand plan or another. When she spotted him, she called out in delight "Lachlan!". Despite her maddening ability to involve herself in his life, Lachlan adored his mother and shared a bond with her that he and Lewis, the head of the family, had not ever reached.

Swept into a warm hug Lachlan greeted his mother. "Are you hassling the help again Dawn?" His tone was mischievous, but his mother stared back at him horrified.

"Don't be such a snob,' she admonished, linking her arm through his and steering him into the large home. "This isn't the damn deep south, and I would never call George the Gardener 'the help'". Lachlan thought she might actually be a little offended, but he couldn't resist a further quip.

"How does Mr Baros like being called 'George the Gardener' though, huh?" He cocked his head at her, and she swatted his arm.

"You can be quite the asshole Senator Wolfe," she retorted, in a prim voice, but the smile on her lips showed her delight in his arrival.

Once inside the spacious house, Dawn hurried off to wash her hands and Lachlan greeted Marg, who was busy in the gleaming kitchen, preparing a vast roast luncheon. Sunday lunches prepared by Marg was a Wolfe family tradition, and since the easing of the virus Lachlan and his sister had missed few; it seemed both he and Sara were recently able to better value their fortunate lives, and Sundays had become something he looked forward to, despite usually battling some sort of hangover from the weekend. Dipping his pinkie finger into the gravy he tasted the rich sauce and moaned appreciatively. Marg reached across and swiped a tea towel at him. "I hope your bloody hands are clean," she hissed at him, but the sparkle in her eyes and smile on her lips belied her amusement.

"No need to whisper," Lachlan whispered back. "Madam just called me an asshole." They pair giggled together, as the front door opened again and the thunderous sound of running children echoed along the long hall.

Lachlan could not remember a time when Marg did not work for the Wolfe family, and her generous nature and cheeky spirit had provided a loving background to his childhood.

As his nieces burst into the kitchen Lachlan grabbed them both and swung them into the air, causing shrieks of excitement to burst from them both.

"For God's sake Lachy." The exasperation in his sister's voice was clear as she followed her rambunctious daughters into the gleaming kitchen. "Don't stir them up! The drive in has been non-stop bickering."

As Sara kissed Marg on the cheek, Lachlan lowered the squirming girls to the ground and ushered them outside to play on the manicured lawns. He loved these kids more than he thought possible, but he did not envy Sara all the time; she had just driven into the city from their acreage property, a drive he knew would have taken a couple of hours. The thought of being locked in the car with the girls on a bad day sounded horrific.

"Sorry," he said, hugging her in apology, before holding her out in front of him to study her. "Ok?" Sara shrugged, then offered a small smile. "I will be when you pour some wine into me." Her smirk was trademark, but tired lines creased her forehead. Lachlan was in the dining room, filling glasses when his parents entered the room to join him, followed closely by Sara. He could hear Ava and Bethany squabbling outside the open window, but it did not seem to require any intervention, thank God. He liked playing doting uncle when the girls were in a good mood, was not so keen to be involved in actual discipline.

"Where's Tim?" Lachlan asked as he passed Sara a large glass of Pinot. She accepted it gratefully and offered another slight shrug.

"He's working at the moment but will call in later when they finish up their production meeting." Sarah's husband was a journalist, and even the major newspapers were struggling to stay afloat, amid advertising cancellations as businesses closed during lockdown.

"I suggested to mum that we leave her big announcement till dinner, but she insisted that family only was just fine." She eyed Lachlan over her glass. "She was really weird about it actually. She carried on like a …"

"Pork chop!" Lachlan and Sara spoke in unison, echoing one of Marg's favourite phrases. The oft joked about childhood memory relaxed them both.

"You look tired," Lachlan said.

"You look like shit," Sara quickly retorted, deflecting his unasked question. "Too much drink or too little sleep?"

It was Lachlan's turn to shrug. "Bit of both, I suppose."

"Who was it this time? A celebrity? A model? Did you get a name at least?" Sara's chiding was good-natured, but he detected an edge to her voice and his stricken expression must have given him away.

"Christ, Lachlan," his sister hissed. "It'll drop off one day. You know, one day you'll wake up and suddenly not be so young, or..." she poked him in the chest with one French manicured fingertip for emphasis "... quite so cute."

He moved her hand away and stepped aside to avoid any further lecturing or rib jabbing.

"Give over," he exclaimed. "Let it go while we work out what bombshell mother dearest has to drop." He deliberately spoke loud enough for both parents to look up. Lachlan realised while he and Sara had been furiously whispering, his parents had been holding their own furtive hushed conversation on the opposite side of the room.

At his words Lewis Wolfe stepped away from his wife and strode to the head of the table.

"Don't be disrespectful Lachlan," he said, sitting on the heavy oak chair. "It doesn't become you."

Lewis was two decades older than Dawn, and while he had high standards, they did not extend to vanity, and Lachlan thought he now looked more like thirty years older than his wife. Perhaps more. The strain of operating the vast Wolfe empire during the disruption and chaos of the worldwide disaster that was virus VS-202 had aged him, Lachlan realised with a shock.

"Please," his mother said. "I need to speak to you both, while the children are occupied and before Tim gets here." She too sat at the long dining table.

Sara shot him a glance, but they both moved to the table and sat wordlessly, as requested.

There was a moment of quiet as both siblings watched their mother expectantly, both feeling more than a little confused.

They watched as Lewis reached across and placed his hand on Dawn's, a small gesture of reassurance that Lachlan found instantly touching. His father was not given to showing affection.

"Go on Dawn." Lewis' voice was gentle.

Dawn cleared her throat and when she spoke it was in a fast-paced monotone, as if she felt once she started to speak, she could not possibly allow herself to stop until the tale was told.

And what a tale it was. Lachlan watched her avoid their gaze as she spoke of an unplanned pregnancy, a baby abandoned at birth, and the search from him years later, only to discover it was too late; Dawn's illegitimate son Logan had fallen victim to the pandemic just weeks before she arrived at his doorstep.

Bizarrely Lachlan's first thought was that he had lost a family member to the virus, and a weird sense of relief that he could sympathise with the rest of the world, but of course that was ridiculous - he had not even known of the existence of this half-brother.

This is too surreal to imagine, he thought. His mother leaving a child behind?

"What I did find," Dawn continued, "when I found Logan's home was his wife. His pregnant wife, Tasmin. We have moved her to the city, to one of the High Street apartments, so I can be involved in the baby's life. So *we* can be involved." She met their gaze now, her eyes flicking between her other children. Confession made, she seemed to regain her trademark confidence. She straightened in her seat and squeezed her husband's hand.

"Your father has met Tasmin, and she is a sweet, lovely girl, that I hope you can both meet her again very soon."

"Again?" the siblings spoke their surprise in unison. Dawn cleared her throat delicately.

"I introduced you at the Anderson-Walkers open house." She looked from Lachlan to Sara. "Tasmin, the young girl who arrived during the welcome." Lachlan thought back, but if he was honest these kinds of events bored him, and he only ever attended to please Dawn and progress his political career. He could not recall the girl at all. Fear of the virus meant social distancing was still being practised, even among the secular upper class, and that tended to make mingling quite difficult.

"The girl who hardly spoke?" Sara sounded aghast. "The one I suggested Rita's tutoring to? The one who was considering nursing? What the hell Dawn!"

"I know," Dawn implored. "It was far from ideal, but I wasn't certain either of you were coming and then when you did it was hardly the time to explain all this." She fell quiet and Lachlan felt the weight of expectation to speak.

Luckily for him, his older sister filled the silence.

"I don't know what to say mum." She was eying Dawn differently, Lachlan felt. "I mean, I understand that it was a hard decision back then, but to just walk away. From your own child. From a baby." Dawn visibly stiffened, but to her credit did not interrupt. "I just don't understand how you could do that." Sara looked to her father. "Dad - what did you say when you found out? When did you find out?"

Lewis looked calmly at his daughter, his favourite child, a fact that he struggled – often unsuccessfully - to hide.

"I have always known," he said. "I knew before we married. I knew just after we met. And I was there to witness your mother's sorrow when you were not, so don't you dare ever imply the decision was made easily." His tone brokered no argument, and Sara sat back, deflated, unused to her father's rebuke.

Lachlan cleared his throat. "Ok, so," he clasped his hands together atop the polished surface of the table. "What is the plan next?" Planning and strategy were familiar territory to him, and right now he needed to inject some sort of reality, some sort of control into the situation. "The child - Logan - has…" he struggled for the kindest word "… passed, and the family is to take his wife and child into the fold, correct?" He looked to his father for confirmation, and Lewis nodded. "Do we need any damage control? Do we need to establish paternity? Is there a possibility this is some sort of scam?" He raised a hand, seeing the protest form on his mother's lips. "Sorry mum, just playing Devil's advocate."

Lewis rose and refilled his scotch glass before turning back to the trio.

"Your mother engaged an investigator. We went looking for the child - Logan - not the other way round." The ice clinked in his glass. "Tasmin and her child are part of this family, and it will be up to you both to get used to that." He stood behind Dawn in a gesture of solidarity and placed a hand on Dawn's shoulder. Lachlan saw her lean back into him, a barely perceptible movement, as if she needed his strength. Lewis looked at Sara and his expression softened. "We have been blessed with two beautiful grandchildren already and now we will welcome a third."

He looked at Lachlan and his tone returned to the brusque business-like manner he was known for. "I have worked on a press statement that I'd like you to look over. You'll probably want to run it all past your man Harry and get the Party onside before this hits the papers. But one thing I know," he looked down at Dawn with that unfamiliar expression of love. "This is something to be celebrated, not swept under the carpet."

The room fell silent, and as if on cue Marg entered the room, carrying a tray of steaming salmon and brightly coloured steamed vegetables, which she placed carefully in the centre of the table.

"I'll go get the girls," Sara mumbled, pushing her chair back and fleeing the room. Dawn watched her leave, a sadness in her eyes, but a bright smile pasted on her face, for Marg's benefit, Lachlan assumed. That was futile; Marg knew more about the tangles of this family than the rest of them combined.

Nothing like another eventful Wolfe family gathering, Lachlan thought wearily. He needed another drink.

The next two weeks flew by in a rush of meetings and briefings, as the country slowly ground back into action following the lockdown. Representatives from the Health Department had beaten a track to his door, in their constant attempts to gain his agreement for further vaccine funding, and despite the Party's conservative position Lachlan could not help but sympathise. The rollout of the vaccine was slow, much slower than predicted, and it did not sit well with him; if ever there was a need for haste it was now. The medication and vaccine stocks were piling up as manufacturers beefed up production, but the hold up was getting trained staff out into the community to administer the vaccines; the Department had lost so many front-line workers to the pandemic that there was now a nation-wide shortage of nurses and doctors. This meant a complicated deal between the unions and the Education Department, to fast-track qualifications and pull in recently retired health care workers, but it was all proving expensive, and the Treasury was screaming.

What's new, Lachlan thought, as he ignored yet another phone call. He was trying to read a weighty medical report, but the technical detail blurred on the page in front of him, until he tossed it aside in frustration. He would have a staffer read it and fill him in on the key points.

God, he was tired. Since the surprise announcement by Dawn more than a fortnight ago he had constantly fielded email and calls from both his mother and sister, who seemed unable to communicate, and so had appointed him their unwilling mediator.

Last night he had ignored both work and family and headed to his private club with a few like-minded colleagues. He joined the rowdy group as they downed expensive scotch in single fiery swallows, until he had felt the tension release from his neck and shoulders. Only then had he allowed his eyes to wander around the dim lounge, until he spied a tall Amazonian brunette with large, high breasts and a silk dress that clung to every curve.

Lachlan had doubted she was wearing any underwear and within the hour he confirmed his suspicions. She had accepted his invitation into one of the club's suites without question and before he had loosened his tie, she had shimmered the swatch of silk to the floor. She had crossed the room, wearing only her patent stilettos, and pushed him back into a plush armchair. When Lachlan emerged for air several hours later, the woman had gone, for which he was extremely grateful; this one did not even leave a card, which was even better. She clearly had no expectations, which was a refreshing surprise.

It was not that Lachlan did not respect women - he believed in treating everyone fairly - but he did not want any long-term commitment. He enjoyed his bachelor life, despite the empty moments, and stubbornly refused to think about a time in the future when those empty moments might fill his entire day. Life was for living, and as long as everyone knew

where they stood, then he planned to enjoy as much
of it as possible.

He was paying for the scotch and bedroom acrobatics
today though. His thighs ached from the intricate
positions they had rolled through, and he was almost
certain they had used every inch of that poor
bedroom. His head had that familiar post-binge ache,
and he was tired, bone tired. Tonight, he would be
heading straight home for a workout then some sleep.
His phone vibrated on the desk, so he flipped it over,
and swiped the screen to reveal a text message from
his mother.

"Dinner tonight at 7pm to meet Tasmin. Sorry for the
late notice but I checked with Harry, and you have no
other appointments. See you then x"

Lachlan cursed aloud, thankful the video call he was
on was muted, and that his image on the screen was
just one thumbnail amongst dozens. Damn Harry - he
had specifically instructed him to not ever accept any
evening invitation without checking. Not even from
Dawn. Especially from Dawn.

He pressed a button on the desk phone and curtly
asked his assistant to come in. The door opened
promptly and as Lachlan lowered the volume on yet
another health official, Harry sat in the leather chair
opposite the Senator.

"Don't sit," Lachlan did not bother to keep the
impatience from his voice, as Harry awkwardly rose to
his feet, his suit-clad rear end having barely touched

the cushion. "Why did you accept an invitation from Mrs Wolfe for this evening?"

Harry, a 30-something with a stellar resume and university degree in political science, but a nervous, timid disposition, reddened obviously.

"I thought …" he began, but Lachlan interrupted, his face stony.

"No Harry. You did not think. I have told you many, many times - unless it is official Party business or a request from the Prime Minister, every single other invitation must come to me."

"I am sorry Senator," The twin red spots on Harry's cheeks only served to infuriate Lachlan further. "I did not accept anything. Mrs Wolfe simply asked me to check your diary to see if you were free, so I thought …"

Lachlan held up a hand to stop his assistant, who fell silent as he hovered anxiously beside the oak desk.

"When it comes to Dawn, that is the same thing." He sighed and tapped the computer to again raise the volume on the meeting that should have his full attention. "Do not do it again. No matter who it is." He dismissed Harry with a flick of his hand, and the assistant scurried quickly to escape.

As the speakers on the screen continued to spout medical information and mortality rates facts, Lachlan's mind wandered into dangerous territory - Kate.

His former PA ran rings around Harry in every way, and Lachlan missed her more than he would ever admit. Whenever his mind meandered backwards to memories of their time together - even the months before their affair had begun - he usually slammed it closed and shut those memories down. But sometimes, in his weakest moments, he allowed his mind to wander back, and every time it was still just as painful. He definitely missed her efficiency and her knowledge of the intricate environment of the House of Parliament, but he also missed her; he missed Kate. He had not expected to still yearn for their deep conversations, and the way she refused to kowtow to him, despite his status. He had not expected to still ache for her touch, despite pushing every memory away as he reached for strangers in the dark.

It was more than a year since she had resigned and - much to his shame - on a few occasions he had resorted to searching her name on the internet to find out where she was now, like a lovesick 12-year-old. The search had delivered only scant information; a new position within the rebuilding program for the State Government, and a social media profile that was private and locked down. It had allowed him access only to a smiling profile picture of her, with a tanned man and two children, posing happily in front of a sloppily decorated Christmas tree. He had instantly regretted clicking that link, but at least he knew - she had gone back to her family, without any hesitation or second thought.

His only saving grace was that no matter how many times he had punched her number into his phone he had not weakened and had not sent one text message nor made one ill-fated call. Lachlan wonders if he will ever see her again but is resigned that the possibility is low.

He, on the other hand, was a stressed wreck of a man, trying to juggle the mess the pandemic had left in its wake and appease the Party elders who held the key to his re-election. Without their support he would be done, and Lachlan feared - deep down - that without his position in the Senate he would be aimless.

His only outlets were the punishing workouts he and his personal trainer pushed his body through, and the nights that passed in a blur of alcohol and random women, but even then, he could not truly be himself. He knows - sad as it is - that the last time he was truly honest and spoke without pause was with Kate.

And now, he had his mother's bombshell to deal with, alongside his sister's unexplainable anger at the situation, and the whole thing was exhausting. It seemed his life was a complicated game of chess, that he was meant to be able to take part in, but the rules just kept changing. The constant pressure made him feel both irritable and unsettled.

He picked up his phone with a sigh to reply to Dawn, but in a pique of childishness decided against it. Let her hang, he thought. Let her guess if I am coming, all the while knowing full well, he would be there.

Lachlan was late, deliberately so, having worked on the vaccine briefs until the last moment, then stopping along the way to grab a bunch of pale pink roses from a florist on the street. He parked his sleek sedan close to the front door beside Sara and Tim's four-wheel-drive wagon and let himself in, the rose scent filling the photo lined hall. As he moved into the house the fragrance of the flowers was joined by a delicious spiciness wafting from the kitchen, and when he reached the kitchen, he found Marg serving large helpings of steaming lasagne onto plates.

"Lasagne?" The question in his voice was obvious as he briefly kissed Marg on one waiting cheek. "Dawn doesn't eat carbs, or have I missed something?"

Hearty, comforting meals were not Marg's usual fare, although, as teens, he and Sara had enjoyed some wonderful nights, eating homemade pizza, creamy pasta, and ice cream sundaes in the kitchen with Marg whenever their parents were away.

"Your mother asked Miss Tasmin what she would like, and lasagne was the suggestion, so that is what you are having." She indicated the lounge room that adjoined the dining room with an inclination of her head.

"You'd best head in. Mr Wolfe has been grumbling about your tardiness, so go sort it out please Lachy. And play nice - don't poke the bear unnecessarily."

Her words were delivered with kindness, but the intent was unmistakable - do not argue tonight.

When Lachlan entered the room, he felt the tension in the air like a hovering damp mist. He took in Sara's straight spine, as she sat upright on what is usually a very luxurious and comfortable sofa; the way she perched on the edge of the seat, both hands wrapped tightly around the stem of a wineglass made the sofa seem like a bed of nails. Beside her, Tim had at least sat back on the lounge, one loafered foot balanced on the other knee, and an arm outstretched across the back of the chair, but he was unusually quiet. Dawn perched on a single burgundy wingback velvet seat, which Sara and Lachlan dubbed the throne behind her back, but her eyes held a nervous brightness, and she too clutched a wine glass like armour.

Lachlan was unsurprised to note Lewis leaning on the mantle, his usual stance, swirling whiskey in a tumbler. "Hello everyone," he said, crossing the room to plant a polite kiss on Dawn's cheek. "Sorry I am a bit late. It's still bedlam trying to sort these vaccines out."

His father nodded in his direction, and Lachlan turned to his sister and her husband. "Hey you two. How are my girls?" Sara answered with a tight smile but said nothing. Tim rushed in to fill the space, delivering a quick update about a babysitter and two phone calls already from his children.

"Hello. You must be Lachlan." The voice behind him was soft but clear, and Lachlan turned to see a delicate girl, clasping a glass of water, as she rose from her seat.

She was much shorter than he, with slim arms and legs, and a cascade of strawberry blond hair that was tucked behind her ears. Her skin was pale except for a smattering of tiny tan freckles on her nose and as she looked at him expectantly, he saw her eyes were a clear blue. She wore no makeup that he could detect, but her discomfort coloured her cheeks and her full lips were rosy. She wore a simple shift dress that skimmed her rounded stomach. Lachlan tore his eyes away from that full belly, lest he seem rude and stepped forward with an outstretched hand.

"And you must be Tasmin," he said simply, taking her hand and shaking it gently. What else could he say? "These are for you," he said, presenting the dozen blush roses to Tasmin. "I thought I should bring something to welcome you to the... ah... family." The stumble was unmissable, as was Sara's distinct huff behind him.

Tasmin graciously chose to ignore both and accepted the roses with a murmured thanks. As she hugged them to her breast to delicately inhale the sweet scent Lachlan saw that the choice of roses was all wrong. Roses were Lachlan's standard go to - his flower of choice. Skip out during the night? Send roses the next day. Mother's Day? Send roses. The birth of a niece? Deliver a huge bouquet to the hospital suite.

But for Tasmin the pale pink buds, though beautiful, seemed all wrong and he suddenly wished he had taken the time to choose more carefully. He wished he had bought a full bouquet of wildflowers and gum leaves and delicate ferns instead.

CHAPTER 2 - TASMIN

When Lachlan strode into the room Tasmin felt an unrealistic sense of relief. Surely, he of all people would be able to diffuse this dreadful situation and clear the buzzing static that filled the room like a swarm of vicious wasps.

On the sofa Sara sat like she was facing an executioner, barely looking in Tasmin's direction barely looking at anyone in fact and directing her terse answers to feeble small talk to a blank spot on the wall in front of her.

Beside her reclined Tim, her husband, torn between seeming friendly and the loyalty he must feel for his obviously upset wife. Lewis hovered about the room, busying himself with drinks and tutting about Lachlan's delay, while Dawn could not seem to keep her shaking hands nor darting eyes still.

It's all so terribly uncomfortable. Tasmin wished she had not so eagerly accepted Dawn's invitation.

Not enough time has passed; it was much too soon to be crashing through their previously close family like the proverbial bull in a china shop. It is easy for Tasmin - apart from Fairy, her protector and confidant, she had no one else close by. Just Fairy, the Wolfe's and the tiny bundle that was now squirming impatiently inside her, and she was pining to gather a family around her. She cupped her hand protectively over her growing stomach, and fought back the urge to flee, as Lachlan entered the room and introduced himself.

The flowers touched her, and she felt tears prick at her eyes. No one had ever bought her flowers before. Not once. The aroma was sweet and fruity and reminded her of spring, and she was almost reluctant to hand them over to Dawn as the older woman busied about organising a vase.

With Dawn out of the room the mood fell even lower and Tasmin found herself looking at Lachlan, almost pleading with him to do something, say something. Say anything that would help this awful night pass as quickly as possible.

As if taking her cue, Lachlan started a light banter with his brother-in-law, chatting easily about national sports competitions recommencing, without crowds until the vaccine was available, and chiding Sara into sharing the horse riding adventures of his nieces.

Even Lewis seemed to relax a little, and Tasmin marvelled at how easily Lachlan moved the conversation around, manoeuvring the testiness of them all into some semblance of cordiality. He was charming, this Senator Wolfe, and Tasmin had no doubt of his ability to plough past any obstacle in his path.

When Dawn returned with the vase of blooms, she smiled brightly at the group and as she placed the vase in the centre of the dining table, Marg sat down the first plates of rich lasagne.

"Come," Dawn called across the open double doorway. "Come and take a seat."

Sara stood quickly. "I'll help you bring the rest Marg," she said tightly, before hurrying toward the kitchen.

Tasmin watched as a glance passed between Marg and Lachlan before he too headed out of the room.

Marg smiled widely. "Well," she said. "It seems I have my own waitstaff tonight." She flicked a quick wink to Tasmin and followed the siblings.

Dawn led Tasmin to the table, which had been shortened to accommodate just the six chairs needed for tonight's dinner.

"You sit here, Tasmin," she said. "Lachlan will sit here at the end, and I shall sit on the other side of you."

Tim sat down opposite Tasmin, and she wondered if it was a deliberate move on his behalf. If it was, she was grateful for the buffer he provided, to avoid the barbed looks of Sara.

When they returned, Lachlan and Sara placed the meals in front of the others and Marg deposited a large bowl of salad on the table before discreetly departing. Tasmin envied her ability to slip out, almost unnoticed.

Lachlan passed the salad to her. "Dawn tells us you're living in one of the units in High Street. How do you find it?"

Tasmin licked her lips nervously, hyper aware of Sara just metres away, although the older woman was studying her plate intently.

"It's a beautiful apartment. I have never lived in anything so new, so it's all a bit surreal right now. But it's close to the hospital and if all goes well in the next year of two, it's close to the Uni as well."

Tim looked up, interestedly. "What are you thinking of studying?" he asked.

Tasmin passed the salad bowl back to Lachlan and he heaped the greens onto his plate.

"I think I'd like to look at something in health care or social welfare, or some sort of community service course," she says softly. It is still hard to believe that any such opportunity might be available to her now. So much has changed in the past few months.

"I'd like to work with children, and families. I think there may be a lot of work to be done when this is over."

Tim looked at her thoughtfully. "I agree," he said simply, and Tasmin got the feeling he had seen a lot in the past months.

"You're a writer?" she asked him, and from across the table, before Tim could answer, Sara snapped. "A journalist. With The Sentinel. There's a difference."

Her snub was unfriendly and Tasmin shrunk a little in her chair.

Tim placed a hand on his wife's arm as Lachlan stared at his sister with a sharp anger flashing in his eyes.

Dawn lowered her fork to the plate with an audible clink, and Lewis simply said, "Be an adult Sara."

Sara whipped her head to face her father and Tasmin saw Tim's grip tighten on her forearm.

"I'd love to be a writer," he said, breaking the tension and filling the air before Sara could say anything further. "I'd love to write biographies or autobiographies, but all that is on the back burner right now." He injected a forced lightness into his tone. "We just report the hard news, ma'am."

"That must be difficult," Tasmin looked at Tim, and he met her eyes briefly before forcing a smile.

"It's not easy, given everything that has happened, but it will get better." The smile did not reach his eyes, Tasmin noted. "It has to."

The dinner party strained through the weight of the situation the guests found themselves in. Lachlan asked about the investigation to locate Logan and Dawn filled them in, answering her son and son-in-law's questions honestly, but without much detail around the circumstances of her first born's death.

"The virus," she said simply, and everyone fell quiet.

Tasmin noted Sara took no part in the conversation, simply nibbling disinterestedly at the rich pasta dish in front of her and gulping wine with a scary gusto.

When she spoke, it startled Tasmin.

"How far along are you?" Sara did not look in Tasmin's direction, but it is obvious by her harsh tone that she is addressing the stranger in the room.

"24 weeks," Tasmin replied. "A little further than I thought but I have had an ultrasound, and everything seems to be fine." No thanks to Logan, she thinks, but does not say. Logan is dead, and there is no reason to poison this family any further with the truth of their brother's cruelty. No need, either, to open herself up to questions about his death.

"Nice." Sara's dull inflection indicates this is the polar opposite to how she truly feels, so Tasmin remains silent. No one else speaks; they wait, giving Sara the time to continue, and she grabbed the opportunity. She sat back in her seat and finally aimed narrowed eyes at Tasmin, who felt the coolness of the gaze as if it were icy water thrown on her.

"How convenient that you managed to somehow find yourself related to a wealthy family," Sara said. "I mean, you must have known who Dawn was, who Lewis is, and I am sure you took no time at all accepting their help." The venom dripped from the words and a bolt of fear shot through Tasmin as she recognises the sneer in Sara's voice - she sounded just like Logan, and Tasmin shrunk a little further.

"Now you have all the medical attention you need, all the opportunities the Wolfe name can provide, all the attention you could even need." She drained the final mouthful of wine from the glass and looked at Tasmin with distaste. "How. Bloody. Convenient."

"Stop it Sara," Lachlan spoke from beside Tasmin, but neither woman looked at him; their eyes were locked across the table. Sara's were bright with distrust while

Tasmin's showed fear and anxiety. This was a big mistake; Tasmin wished she could flee, wished she had never come.

"You're acting like a brat Sar, so just stop it. None of this is Tasmin's fault." Lachlan's words caused his sister to spin in her seat and face him. Her hand came down hard on the tabletop and Dawn and Tasmin both jumped.

"A brat?" she said. "Fuck you Lachlan. How can you sit there and just accept this is all ok? This will affect your career, and my family. Do you really think I want to share our parents with the child of some nobody? Of someone we don't even know?" She looked at Tasmin again, eyeing her as if she were a piece of litter blown into the gutter, before turning back to Lachlan. "This could all be bullshit." She turned her attention to Lewis. "Surely you will be doing paternity and other DNA testing? How are you protecting yourself? How are you protecting my girls?"

Dawn started to speak, but Sara rudely cut her off with a raised palm. "Don't bother," she said flatly. "This is your mess. You caused this. Aren't we enough for you Dawn? Is that why you need to save ...."

Sara did not finish; Lewis rose from his seat and roared. "Enough!"

The patriarch and his eldest child scowled at each other in the soundless room, before Sara abruptly stood. She wrenched the napkin from her lap and threw it on the table before turning to storm from the room.

Tim also stood and cleared his throat. "I'm sorry," he said simply. He crossed to kiss Dawn on the cheek and squeeze her reassuringly on the shoulder, then shook Lewis' hand firmly.

"I'll speak with her," he said. "She just needs time." Looking across to Tasmin he nodded kindly. "It was really nice to meet you Tasmin. I hope to see you soon." With a quick pat on Lachlan's back, he was gone.

As Lewis returned to his seat, Tasmin released the breath she had not realised she had been holding. Her head felt light, and the uneasy silence was equalled only by the apprehension skittering in her chest. In the few short months since Logan's death, she had forgotten how confrontation and ugliness fizzed fear into her fingertips and how panic stole her breath, but right now she was straight back into that nightmare.

It was Dawn who spoke first. "Tasmin," she began, her voice quiet. "I apologise for Sara's behaviour. I hope you will forgive us. It is quite … unseemly." The tiny tremble in her voice broke Tasmin's heart and she raced around the dining table and threw her arms around the woman without hesitation. Dawn stiffened at first, but after a moment Tasmin felt her soften, before she gratefully hugged the younger woman back.

Later that night Tasmin tried to explain to Fairy what had happened.

"She what?!" Fairy's indignation was palpable even down the phone line, and Tasmin was filled with the warmth of the old woman's protection, as she sat curled on the lounge. The curtains were open and through the windows Tasmin could see the city before her, all the way across to the suburb where she had lived beside Fairy - it seemed like a lifetime ago.

"Tell her to pull her bloody head in," Fairy now said. "Before someone does it for her, upstart bitch." Despite herself Tasmin giggled as she tried to admonish Fairy.

"She just needs time," Tasmin said, echoing Tim's words. Her first instinct on arriving home was to call Fairy and relive the disastrous evening, and already she was feeling better. "She is feeling pretty put out, I'd say, but hopefully she'll come around eventually."

"I thought you told me she seemed nice, that first time you met? She's showing her true colours now." Fairy sounded unashamedly gleeful, and Tasmin scolded her gently. "Enough about the princess," Fairy continued. "Tell me about the Senator. Is he as dishy as he looks on the tele?"

Tasmin laughed out loud. "Oh, he's handsome all right," she agreed. "Trouble is, he damn well knows it. He joked with Tim - that's Sara's husband - about staying up all night before a Senate vote and falling asleep during the debates, so I'm not sure he's anyone we should vote for again."

"I didn't vote for him last time," Fairy admitted. "I only vote for women, you know, to try and even it up a bit." She chuffed at herself. "Was he a dickhead too? Tonight, I mean."

Tasmin recalled the flowers, abandoned at Dawn's in her haste to leave. "No," she said. "He was actually really kind. Very charming, of course, but he was friendly enough. Tim was too, and you've met Dawn and Lewis," Fairy could not disguise the subtle humph at the mention of Dawn's name - the two continued to battle for Tasmin's affection in an exasperating game of cat and mouse.

"Everyone was really nice, considering everything. Everyone except Sara, that is." Tasmin's voice was sad as she realised she had hoped for far more from the evening than she had dared to admit.

CHAPTER 3 - SARA

Sara sat in the luxurious wagon, outside her parent's home, for several minutes before Tim joined her, mortified at her behaviour, yet unable to quell the fury that filled her head.

Wordlessly, Tim carefully closed the heavy front door of her parent's home, before joining her in the car. Her husband did not speak as he reversed from their parking space and drove down the tree lined driveway and onto the main road. She did not speak either - what on earth could she say to justify her behaviour back there?

They shared an uncomfortable 30 minutes of silence before Tim spoke.

"I meant what I said."

Sara was puzzled. She had been expecting him to rip into her for acting like a child and was confused by the words spoken in the dark, as they sped along the highway toward their rural retreat.

"What?" She did not turn to look at him. They both faced forwards, the orange freeway lamps periodically illuminating them, and the white lines on the road sliding silently beneath them.

"What I said. Back there. I would love to be a writer. I know journalism is a good gig and it's not that I'm not grateful to still be working, but I'd love to write properly. You know?"
Sara scoffed "No Tim. I don't bloody know." She instantly regretted her hard words as Tim's hands tightened on the leather steering wheel. Even in the dark she felt him tense, and a deep remorse at her harsh words flooded Sara's heart.
"I'm sorry," she sighed. "I'm so sorry Tim." She wearily ran her hand through her dark hair. "What the hell happened to me back there? Christ I was an asshole. But… I just..."
Tim reached for her hand in the dark and brought it to his lips, kissing her fingertips briefly, interrupting her.
"I think you're scared," he said simply, and Sara scoffed again.
"Don't be ridiculous."
"I'm not. Think about it. You've always been Lewis' golden girl. The high achiever. The Olympian hero. But now, in comes some girl none of us even knew about, the wife of a brother you didn't know about, and your equilibrium has been tilted."
He stole a glance at her now, but Sara refused to turn towards him. Tim sighed.
"I know you are Lewis' favourite. I know it, you know it, even poor bloody Lachy knows it, but that doesn't replace the fact that Dawn is his wife. You love your Dad to bits Sar, but his loyalty is to Dawn, and if

taking Tasmin into the family is something Dawn wants, then of course Lewis will support that."

A hot tear slipped down Sara's cheek, and she was grateful for the darkened interior.

"It may not be what you want to hear sweetheart," Tim continued, taking a deep breath. "But not everything can go your way. You've been the centre of this family your whole life, but it's time you grew up and realised there's more to life than just what you want." Tim's voice was uncharacteristically hard, and his words caused Sara's throat to ache with unshed sobs.

"Fuck you," she said quietly, before turning her back on him to stare out the side window. Neither she nor Tim spoke for the rest of the long, lonely journey.

The space between Sara and Tim was frosty for days following the dinner and drive home. Neither referred to it again, and Tim retreated into his work, spending long hours either at the office or commuting between home and work. His absence made their conflict less obvious and while Sara missed him deeply, it was easier than the way they were ignoring each other when he was home.

She filled the long hours by taking their girls on picnics down to the creek that ran at the bottom of their garden, and for horse rides through the wide brown paddocks that stretched across their 100 acres. The land was really too big for what they needed, but the entire place had been a steal compared to buying in the city, and the sprawling homestead had captured Sara's heart on their very first visit. Back then, it had needed a complete renovation, which she had worked on tirelessly, as a labour of love, as Tim moaned about the cost and Lewis chided her about over-capitalising the property. She had ignored them all and now the home was restored to its former glory, standing proudly amongst lush gardens and verdant lawns. The wide verandah housed rattan furniture and the brickwork had been repaired around each of the floor to ceiling sash windows. Inside, modern comforts, such as central heating, were hidden, allowing the graceful arches and high panelled ceilings to echo a colonial yesteryear. She loved this place, even more so now, as it insulated them from the terror of the pandemic.

When the virus first hit, she and Tim had joked about holing up at Carinya, the name they had given their property, once part of a much larger sheep station. Tim had discovered the Aboriginal word on one of his travels, and its meaning - a happy home - seemed perfect as they had eagerly awaited the birth of Ava, their first daughter, now almost seven.

Bethany had not long turned five, and Sara felt her family was complete, and thanks to Carinya's isolation she had been able to keep them safe during those worst months. Tim had worked from home, and regular deliveries of food and craft or gardening materials meant they had passed the time almost unscathed. Sara knew this was not entirely true, however; Tim was one of the country's leading journalists, and as such, was privy to some of the worst statistics and stories. He and Lachlan had grown even closer, despite the physical distance, as they discussed the fate of them all during many hushed, sorrowful late-night phone calls. On more than one occasion Sara had heard Tim quietly crying after speaking to Lachlan about the latest death toll, and during those worst months, her husband's kind eyes were often red rimmed with anguish. Tim and Lachlan's relationship as brothers-in-law had solidified as they discussed the horrors neither of them wanted her to know. Sara knew her husband was a changed man, deeply affected by the stories of loss and helplessness, but she was grateful for his protection of her and their girls. It was almost shameful, but she did not want to know about everyone else, as long as she could keep her family safe. By ignoring the news, she had been able to convince herself and her daughters that the pandemic was happening elsewhere and would not ever reach them. It was how she had coped. *Be careful what you wish for*, she thinks bitterly. In reality, her family now faced an even bigger threat. This interloper. Tasmin.

Sara refused to believe Tim's words from the car, even though they repeatedly played through her rattled mind. She knew she held a privileged place in her father's heart, but that alone was not a reason to trust this girl or welcome her with open arms. A girl none of them knew, carrying a child everyone expected her to be happy about. Sara insisted - even to herself - that her mistrust was based on a need to protect her family, *their* family, from the potential threat this girl presented.

Sara filled the electric kettle with water and placed it back on its snug hob, flicking the switch before proceeding to prepare herself a coffee. Strong, black, and hot, just how she liked it.

When Sara had been growing up, success and confidence had come easily, and this feeling of seismic upheaval was unfamiliar and altogether unpleasant. Oh, she had put in the hard yards - early mornings, aching muscles and little free time - but these trade-offs had meant her career as a water polo player had simply flourished, as expected. Her success had taken effort, but she had never really doubted she would succeed. She and Lewis had set their sights on the 2004 Olympics in Greece before she had finished secondary school studies, and the announcement of her inclusion in the team was gracefully accepted by them both, as fate shone upon her, as planned.

The Australian team fared well at the Games, winning their pool, and narrowly missing out on the bronze medal, but the team's performance served her exceptionally well. She became a news story as the team progressed beyond expectations; the daughter of a captain of industry and charity queen, meant Sara literally became the poster child of the Australian Olympic team.

She graced the cover of a popular women's magazine, her lithe body clad in the national flag, her sunny smile flashing perfect teeth, beaming from newsstands across the country. From there she secured a well-known agent to the stars and became a sought-after sports commentator and motivational speaker.

At one boozy lunch in aid of a cancer hospital, Sara found herself seated beside an interesting man, furiously scribbling notes in some sort of alien script, on a small pad beside the polished silverware.

He nodded her a brief, distracted greeting when she sat in the vacant seat beside him, as guests hurried to their seats as the emcee started the formalities. She chatted across the linen clad round table, leaning closer to the stranger in an attempt to speak to the other guests, around the large floral centrepiece obscuring their view. She was mildly miffed when the man leaned away to give her more room.

Eventually, the emcee called her name and she rose from her seat, and moved through the room, stopping briefly at the tables of those she knew in the room, the biggest movers and shakers, and the ones she hoped would bid obnoxious amounts of money in the auction that followed. When she reached the podium she began her talk, confident in her ability to capture the audience. She spoke about the climb to the pinnacle of sporting achievement and peppered her speech with anecdotes of famous sportspeople and life at the Olympic village. She had practised the speech several times and rarely consulted her notes. Instead, she treated the many guests as if they were friends, and indeed many were, and she rode the wave of applause back to her table.

The stranger in the seat beside now looked at her with recognition. He offered his hand, and she shook it, glad he gripped it firmly. Like an equal.

"I'm sorry," he began. "I didn't realise I was sharing a table with the headline act."

She smiled. "Hardly headline," she said, but they both knew that was untrue. She had been contracted by the event organiser to pull in the big money guests and boost the fundraising coffers of the hospital. "You now know who I am, and yet I have no idea who I am fortunate to be sharing lunch with."

She liked the look of this man, despite herself, and saw no need to be coy. He seemed to be a similar age to her, she estimated. His hairline had receded, and his hair was cut quite short, as if he had no time bothering to hide the fact he was balding, but it suited him. His face was unlined, save some shallow laugh lines at his eyes. The stubble on his chin and cheeks was shot through with grey, but it was neatly manicured, and his suit was a classic well-cut affair. Despite his quiet style, he was not her usual type. Sara was usually drawn to good looking, sporty types, with windswept hair and buff, tanned limbs, and her interest surprised her. Perhaps it was the thrill of not being recognised.

"Tim Byrnes," he introduced. "I work at The Sentinel, but I am covering for my Editor, which is why I am at the good table." He grinned, and Sara watched as the

smile danced mischievously in his eyes. "His loss looks
like it's my gain."

They talked throughout the auction, to the exclusion
of all the other guests at their table, something Sara's
mother would have chided her for. When the
luncheon ended, they moved into the dim bar, and
talked some more. They sipped chilled Sauvignon
Blanc from the Riverina, and discussed politics, their
families, the state of pre-school education and their
favourite movies. They quizzed each other about
music and Christmas traditions and before Sara knew
it, it was approaching midnight and the lounge bar had
emptied.

Tim did not ask to come home with her that evening,
but emailed her the next day, via her agent and they
met at an inner-city jazz club for a late meal. The next
day Sara emailed him and proposed a trip to the zoo
that weekend, and very quickly they realised that
something meaningful was developing.

They fell into an easy, comforting love. A courtship
encouraged by both families, despite their surprise - on
paper Sara and Tim should not be compatible, yet they
complimented each other as if they had been together
for years. Sara was confident to the point of being
brash, while Tim was more considered and
empathetic, but with Sara at his side he was less
cautious. Sara had the time and connections to
support Tim to build his career, and Tim taught her
how to enjoy the simple pleasures. He introduced her

to snow skiing, and she joined his family during their epic winter holiday Monopoly marathons.

Their engagement seemed a foregone conclusion, a natural progression to their adoration of each other, and their wedding was featured in the society pages of each of the national weekend papers.

That blush of love seemed extremely far away today, as Sara filled the ceramic mug with boiling water and breathed in the rich aroma of coffee and regret.

CHAPTER 4 - TASMIN

Two days later an email pinged its arrival and when Tasmin opened her phone, she was surprised to see it was from Lachlan.

"Hello Tasmin,

I'm deeply sorry about the other night and I am hoping you'll allow me to take you to lunch tomorrow to help make up for it.

I have a standing reservation at Vito's, in the city, not far from your apartment.

Can we say 1pm? Let me know if you are available.

Regards,

Lachlan"

Tasmin stared at the email, re-reading it. Available? Of course she was. The city was still recovering and although she felt somewhat cocooned from the most disastrous effects of the pandemic now, her social calendar was hardly full. Her days consisted of obstetrician appointments, applying surprisingly fiddly jungle animal motifs to the walls of the nursery and binge-watching dramas on television.

Her availability was not the issue; it was not a matter of could she, and more a matter of should she? Sara's treatment of her was still very raw and Tasmin was hesitant to expose herself, or the baby for that matter, to any further stress inducing anger. Sara's vitriol had shaken Tasmin to the core.

Unable to decide, Tasmin instead opened the web browser on her phone and searched for Vito's. Images of mouth-watering morsels filled her screen and she read through the menu with amazement - this was not a place she had ever experienced. After just a moment of hesitation, she quickly typed out an acceptance email and sent it whirling through the ether to Senator Wolfe's office.

Almost instantly a reply came back. "Shall I send a car for you?"

Tasmin consulted the maps function of her smartphone, before flicking off her own reply.

"No thank you. It is quite close, and I'd enjoy the walk. I will see you tomorrow. T."

She then dialled Fairy. "You'll never guess where I am going!"

CHAPTER 5 - LACHLAN

When Lachlan entered the cosy Italian bistro that was his favourite place to relax and entertain, the maître d greeted him warmly. Usually, he joined his mother or Sara and Tim here, or one of the mates from Uni when they visited town. This was not where he brought a date - those liaisons were best suited to sleek modern restaurants or smoky bars - which is why Vito's was the first place he thought to suggest to Tasmin.

He was surprised to see her before him, already seated at the small dark table towards the back, the one that overlooked the river below. Lachlan chuckled to himself - clearly the staff assumed she was some sort of paramour, and had given them a discreet, private location.

Tasmin looked up as he approached, and Lachlan was struck by how naturally beautiful she was. Not sexy - not at all, he admonished himself - but her pale skin seemed somehow silky and her hair, with its loose, free falling coppery waves were in stark contrast to the stiff, shellacked hair styles of the other women in the restaurant.

"Hello," she said simply.

"Hi," Lachlan replied, sitting down as a waiter appeared at his side. "I hope you haven't been waiting long?"

She shook her head quickly. "Not really. I walked here, so I kind of, you know, just wandered, window shopping and people watching, until I made it to here." She shrugged her slight shoulders. "I'm still getting to know my way around."

The waiter beside them cleared his throat quietly and Lachlan started.

"Oh, drinks. Yes. Tasmin? What would you like? A wine?" He reddened at his error as Tasmin looked down to the timber tabletop. "Of course not." *What the hell was he thinking, offering a pregnant woman wine. For Christ's sake!*

Unexpectedly flustered Lachan ordered a freshly squeezed juice for them both, then busied himself with the menu. Lunch selections made, the waiter left them, and it was Tasmin that spoke first.

"This is very nice of you Lachlan," she began. "But there is no need to make up for anything you think Sara has done." Her voice was quiet, and Lachlan leant forward to better hear her. She did not meet his eyes, not directly, but continued determinedly. "Sara is entitled to feel however she feels. There is no right or wrong in all this." Again, her shoulders lifted slightly, resignedly. "It is understandable that she is angry, and I am sorry for that. I won't be visiting the house again, and I have already told Dawn." A small smile played on her lips. "I don't think you mother is much used to being told anything."

Lachlan laughed out loud, leaning back in the seat, grateful the conversation had elevated away from how dreadfully his sister had treated this girl.

"Now that's an understatement." The pair smiled hesitantly at each other.

"Look," he said, trying to be business-like, but failing. "This is a weird situation for everyone, yourself included, but that doesn't explain Sara's outburst the other night and I just hope you believe me when I tell you she is usually a really great person." He paused, searching for a way to express their closeness without sounding too dramatic. "Growing up she was my protector, actually she still is. We are very close, so maybe she is still trying to protect the family." Lachlan saw a look of dismay pass across Tasmin's face. "Not that we need protecting from you!" he said hurriedly. *God he was making a mess of this.*

"Anyway, I just want you to know she will come around, and in the meantime, you have the rest of us to rely on." Eager to move away from such a mushy, emotive conversation, Lachlan changed the subject just as the wait staff placed their lunches in front of them. He reached for a large slice of the trademark Vito's pizza, his all-time favourite indulgence, and said, "Tell me about you and Logan."

Tasmin had just lifted her cutlery and the silverware clattered noisily to the table, as she lost her grip.

"Oh," she seemed agitated. "I'm so sorry. I'm such a klutz." Lachlan could see a panicked wildness in her eyes.

"Are you ok?" he asked. "Is it the baby?" It is the first time he has broached the subject, that sat roundly between them.

"What? Oh, no, I'm fine. Just clumsy." She retrieved her fork and stabbed at the salmon salad in front of her. Lachlan munched on his slice of gooey pizza as she composed herself. *She is always apologising,* he thought.

They eat in silence until Tasmin appeared to steel herself sufficiently to speak.

"Logan and I met when I was working as a pharmacy assistant and we fell in love," she said simply. "I stopped working when we got married but Logan worked in security, mainly nightclub doorman jobs, that kind of thing. Of course, all that stopped when the virus hit, and we went into lockdown. Our part of the city locked down more than once if you remember."

Lachlan remembered all right; he was part of the machine that made the decision to put the western suburbs back into extended isolation three times, to protect the city centre. *And the wealthy waterfront suburbs,* he admitted, but only to himself.

"What about the, uh, illness? Were you able to get him to a treatment centre?", Lachlan asked, referring to the satellite centres established in stadiums and empty universities across the country.

Tamsin shook her head. "No," she said simply. "It was very quick."

"But you were not …"

Tasmin cut him off. "No. I was able to move in with Fairy, my neighbour, so stayed safe." She absentmindedly caressed her stomach. "Luckily."

Lachlan found her lack of emotion worrying but had no way of knowing how people dealt with trauma, having escaped the worst of the pandemic. He had heard stories from frontline workers and read all the reports, but God only knows what it had been really like, for those who lost loved ones.

"Can you tell me more about him? About Logan?" Lachlan could not explain why, but he had a need to know more about this brother he had not known existed.

Instantly the fear flashed across Tasmin's face, and Lachlan watched her struggle to carefully arrange a calm expression.

"Oh, he was wonderful," she said, without hesitation. "An awfully hard worker. Very ambitious."

The lack of detail puzzled Lachlan, and he had cross-examined enough colleagues and staffers to know when someone was hiding something.

"What about your family," he asked instead. "Where are they?"

This time Tasmin's smile was instantaneous and genuine.

"I have a sister living in New Zealand, and once …" she paused, searching for the right word to explain that dreadful time. "… things started getting really bad, she sent for my parents. They are still over there with her now, loving being honorary Kiwis." Her face softened with affection and Lachlan is struck anew with how lovely she looked when she smiled.

"Yes, New Zealand really did well during the whole pandemic, didn't they?" He cannot keep the regret from his voice. "We should have moved quicker." Looking at her he added "But I'm glad to hear your family is safe. You weren't tempted to go too?" Despite his official political stance Lachlan could not fault those who managed to flee to the safety of the neighbouring country. For many, the decision likely saved their lives.

A cloud passed across Tasmin's pale face once more. "No," she said simply. "We decided to stay here." The dull tone makes Lachlan believe the decision may not have been hers.

CHAPTER 5 - TASMIN

The lunch was a pleasant surprise. To be honest, the lure of an award-winning meal at Vito's had been the driving force to accept Lachlan's invitation, but Tasmin had been pleasantly surprised at how much she enjoyed the afternoon.
As she wandered back along tree-lined streets, in a city still only just emerging from lockdown, she mused over their encounter.
Lachlan was a curious revelation. She had expected the confident statesman to be rather shallow beyond his obvious charm, but the few hours spent with him had revealed an intelligent, well-read man. They had discussed their favourite writers and discovered a shared love for the father of horror Stephen King, but the most unanticipated discovery was unearthing Lachlan's angst at the state of the nation. The vulnerability he had shown when slowly speaking about the challenges the Government faced to move out of the pandemic had touched Tasmin. The exposure to this caring nature was something Lachlan admitted he dare not show too often, lest it come across as weakness to political rivals.

"Our own Party is often the worst," he had admitted to her, his voice soft and thoughtful. "There is such an expectation of projecting a strong, stern persona. The exact opposite of what all the research tells us voters actually want to see from us." His frustration had been clear. "People want us to be honest and calm yet understanding, but the Party just wants us all to strike fear in voters. Fear of what could happen if they vote for the other blokes. It's all backwards," he had finished, with a sigh.

Tasmin found his honesty engrossing and the fact he spoke so freely with her - as if her opinion mattered - was intoxicating. Years of being belittled and demeaned into that small fibro clad home by Logan had ripped away all confidence in herself, and yet after just a few hours with Lachlan, Tasmin felt revived. She felt valued, for the first time in a very long time.

She made her way across the street, crossing midway, as the traffic was still slow enough to allow her to avoid the intersection, with its pedestrian lights and beeping alarm. Even though the daytime lockdown restrictions had lifted in the city, the business district was much slower, sleepier, and people kept a wary distance from each other. Lachlan had explained that companies had invested so heavily in equipping their workforces to labour from home, or smaller suburban offices, that they were cautious about re-filling the CBD skyscrapers. They had discussed the work life balance, something Tasmin had not had the luxury of considering, living in a constant state of terror a few months ago, but both she and Lachlan agreed that the pandemic offered some new solutions to stressed, overworked parents. Entire industries had proven that working at home, in hastily organised dining room workstations, was not only possible, but it was also remarkably productive.

Lachlan had shared with her that he was quietly working with researchers, collecting data to support further Government investment in telecommunications, so that working from home could become the new normal.

"Imagine giving everyone those commute hours back," Lachlan had said, as they lingered over aromatic Vito coffees, his eyes twinkling. "I have colleagues who now exercise - with their kids in tow - before work and faff about in vegie gardens in the evenings." Tasmin wanted to ask how much of his childhood Lewis had shared but held back. They did not know each other well enough for such an intimate question. She felt she already knew the answer, having spent just one agonising evening with the Wolfe clan.

He had laughed then and named a senior MP, often quoted in the media for his hard-line rants against social welfare reform. Tasmin nodded at the name - even she had heard of him and his legendary tantrums in Parliament.

"He keeps chickens." Lachlan had continued to laugh at her astonished expression. "I kid you not. He has chickens and grew so many zucchinis that he shared them with neighbours - this is the North Shore remember, so how ridiculous would that sentence have been this time last year! - so got to know the Greek magnate up the road." He had sipped his long black seriously then. "Just talking to this one family - who are mega rich themselves - meant old Joe has heard first-hand accounts from refugees, and discussed the support services the Greek guy has set up for staff … childcare centres, subsidised housing … stuff like that." He placed his cup on the table and shrugged. 'You know, all the things the Government should be taking care of. Anyway, I do believe that the pandemic has taught us a lot about the value of using time more wisely and opened up all sorts of conversations among people used to avoiding each other" He had rolled his eyes exaggeratedly, but Tasmin could see he was cramped by his Party. Secretly, she was thrilled at being privy to such information. It was electrifying to be trusted with some of the intricacies of Lachlan's work.

The pall over the day was his eagerness to learn more about Logan. His questions had thrown her into a paralyzing panic, and she had felt the old anxiety gripping her as she struggled to answer. What could she tell him? How could she impart such pain on this man, who only seemed to want to do good, no matter how deeply he hid it.

It was different discussing Logan with Dawn. Since Fairy's outburst, she had been honest with Dawn about her late husband's temper, traumatic childhood,

and addiction, and if she had asked directly, Tasmin
would have told her about his death too.

She and Fairy had discussed it, during the frantic time
following Dawn's arrival at their door, the day she had
come looking for her lost son. Fairy had pleaded with
her to keep the secret, but Tasmin had been adamant;
if Dawn asked, she would tell her it was she who was
responsible for his death, and she meant it.

Tasmin knew that admitting to such a crime would not
only alienate Dawn, but also cost her her freedom, but
she would not lie.

"As long as I can make sure this baby is cared for, I
don't really care what happens to me," she had told
Fairy. She knew enough of Dawn now to hope she
would take this child without hesitation, should
Tasmin be gaoled, and as they got to know each other,
she had waited with jangled nerves for Dawn's
questions or accusation.

Except they never came. She and Dawn had many
difficult conversations about Tasmin's life with Logan,
the way he controlled her life, their money and how
his rage escalated as the drugs took further hold. She
held nothing back. Tasmin told Dawn of the injuries,
the intimidation and the dread that filled her every
waking moment, even before the virus entered their
collective lives.

"One day I woke, and he was standing over me with a
knife. He lunged and stabbed the bed beside me." As
Tasmin recalled the terrifying moment, she was
thrown back in time. She could smell his fetid

cannabis breath as he leaned closer to her. "He had been upset for days following our work Christmas party, accusing me of flirting with my boss Mr Cartwright and he told me no man would want me once he scarred my face. I quit work after that."

Dawn had cried noiselessly, heaping guilt upon guilt at the way Logan had acted. How much of his behaviour was due to his upbringing? How much of this was her fault? To Tasmin it seemed she accepted all this as her sin, and her penance was to avoid asking any direct questions about Logan's death.

During one such conversation Tasmin could bear it no longer, and despite Fairy's pleading warnings, she had taken a deep breath, intent on explaining her role in Logan's demise. Tasmin still had no doubt that it had been a case of him or her; she knew that either the violence would have escalated to a point he killed her, or his addiction would have made him careless, and the virus would have consumed them both.

"Dawn," she had said. "There is something I need to tell you. About Logan's death. I ..."

Dawn had quickly placed a hand on Tasmin's, gripping it with enough force to stop the words.

"Let's not talk about that," she had said, and so they had not.

Tasmin knew Dawn had shared her experiences with Lewis. When he and Dawn moved her and her meagre belongings to the apartment, he had quietly but affectionately placed a hand on her shoulder before he left.

"You will be safe here," he had said simply, and with that Tasmin knew he knew the truth, or part of it, at least.

But their children had no idea of the ordeal of Logan's dark childhood, and there seemed no reason to enlighten them, and further punish an already anguished Dawn. However, now she was getting to know Lachlan, and it was only natural he wanted to know more about a brother only recently revealed. Hopefully, she would be able to paint a favourable enough picture of a fantasy sibling, for Lachlan and Sara, even if the words stuck in her throat, like a suffocating mass of lies.

CHAPTER 7 - LACHLAN

Lachlan sent a text message to his sister. "When are you in town next? Let me take you to dinner." He watched the three dots dance on the screen of his smartphone, indicating she was writing an immediate response.

"Not anytime soon." She was fobbing him off, Lachlan realised, frustrated.

Sitting at his vast desk in his office in the House he drummed his fingers thoughtfully before punching the intercom and rousing his assistant.

Harry answered immediately. "Yes Senator?"

"What is on today?"

Harry rattled off a to do list of meetings and tasks that would fill the next ten or so hours. Lachlan decided none of it was overly pressing so directed a stunned Harry to reschedule it all, save one phone conference due to commerce within the hour.

"Divert that to my mobile phone," he instructed. "I'll be travelling long enough to deal with that, but make sure the call is recorded and have the transcript emailed to me later today."

He released the button and stood, before pressing the intercom once again.

"Thanks Harry. I appreciate it," he added.

As expected, the traffic was light and once the teleconference was done, Lachlan relaxed into the drive to Sara's. He arrived in good time and found his sister and nieces in the lounge room, engrossed in a primary school zoom class. When lockdown forced the country inside their homes, and schools across the nation closed, Sara became one of the millions of parents thrust into the role of teacher. Like many, she panicked at this new position as educator and overcompensated by converting their vast TV into a video chat screen. It had been a lifeline for Lachlan too, and he often called the girls to catch up when they physically were not able to. The large format meant they could more easily scramble over each other to show him their artworks, their spindly flower seedlings and their menagerie of pets, and these calls had helped keep them all sane.

The calls had offered Sara a respite from the 24/7 pressure of entertaining the girls and reminded Lachlan that the world was not all lost. *God, he had need that back then.*

Ava and Bethany screamed when they saw him and flung themselves at him, as Sara hastily grappled with the remote to mute the chaos, for the benefit of the other students. She allowed the trio a few moments of loving jostling, before ushering the girls back to the lesson – officially it was Ava's class, but thankfully it enthralled Bethany too. She pushed Lachlan towards the kitchen, closing the door behind them.

She was quiet as she busied herself in the long galley kitchen, gleaming with expensive appliances and stone benchtops. Lachlan sat at the long island bench and looked around. It seemed Sara had been rage cleaning, a habit that she and Dawn shared, although Dawn was now more apt to undertake a renovation or garden makeover, ruthlessly bullying tradesmen and landscapers until spent. While financially comfortable, Sara and Tim did not share such wealth, so when she was stressed, or angry, Sara cleaned. With vigour.

Lachlan cleared his voice. He had not driven this far not to get this over with.

"How you doing?" he enquired.

Her back to him Sara answered. "Fine."

He sighed. "Don't be a shit, Sar. This is me. How are you, really?" He hoped he had kept the embarrassing whine from his voice. Despite enjoying ruthless debates in his work life, he hated when the family was unsettled.

She turned now and faced him. Leaning back against the designer kitchen and crossed her arms across her chest and glared at him.

Uh-oh, thought Lachlan. *So not good then.* Her combative stance said it all.

"I'm angry," she said. "What did you expect? I didn't want to talk about this, I *don't* want to talk about it, which is why I said I wasn't coming into the city, and yet here you are." Her words tumbled from her, so Lachlan did not interrupt.

"I don't trust this girl. I hate what Dawn is putting us through, and I can't stand how eager you and Tim are to play happy families." The final words were spat in his direction with such venom that Lachlan was momentarily taken aback.

"Whoa," he said. "No one is playing at anything Sara. This is very real, and something we have to deal with, the best we can. No point hiding out here with your head in the sand."

She scoffed and turned back to the coffee machine, thumping mugs from the cupboard and tapping one foot impatiently as the water gurgled to boiling point. From his vantage point Lachlan could see her jaw bones clenching. He tried again.

"I had lunch with her yesterday and I don't think life has been easy for her." Sara was unresponsive so he ploughed on. "I think this Logan might not have been the ideal husband, not that she has said anything; it's more of a feeling I get when she speaks about him. It's like she's scared or something." Still Sara said nothing, and Lachlan watched her cautiously until she poured thick coffee into the mugs and crossed the short distance to hand him a steaming cup. The wide island bench separated them, but Lachlan felt much more was keeping them divided, apart from the slab of imported stone. Their emotional distance felt like an aching chasm.

He tried again. "C'mon Sar. You can't keep this up forever."

Sara regarded her brother coolly. "And what exactly am I 'keeping up', Lachlan? I am the only member of this family that is taking this … situation … seriously. I am the only one not instantly head over heels with the new arrival." Her chest was heaving, and Lachlan was again surprised at the vitriol behind her words. "You come here, to my home, when I obviously DID NOT want to deal with this today, all doe eyed and long eyelashes, but you forget Lachlan - I am NOT one of your stupid bimbos. I don't fall for your charming, empty bullshit, and I can see through your visit."

Lachlan began to protest; he wanted Sara to understand he was here for her, for the girls, for their parents, but his sister seemed uninterested in his stuttering attempts to calm her.

"You've never worked hard for a single thing, Lachlan," she said cruelly. "You have had a leg up or a handout every single day of your life, and this is no different. You haven't even taken the time to consider all this, yet here you are, doing mummy's bidding. Arriving on my doorstep to convince me Tasmin will not ruin this family." Lachlan was shocked into silence, but Sara still had much to say.

"You aren't here to check in on me. You're here to make YOURSELF feel better. God forbid, something might not go to plan in your perfect movie script life."

As she continued her emotive ranting, Lachlan stared at her with disbelief. The woman before him was a stranger to Lachlan. Her lips were set in such a tight line the colour had been squeezed from them, and hot, angry tears glinted in her normally kind eyes. Her posture was rigid, held up by an anger he could not comprehend.

This was a mistake.

Lachlan heard the girls bidding a noisy goodbye to classmates in the nearby room and knew he needed to stem the flow of hatred before they raced into the kitchen. He stood, pushing his untouched coffee toward Sara.

"I don't know what the hell is going on with you Sara, but I don't deserve any of this." He wanted to rail at her, tear layers from her heart as she had just done to him, but he would not ever expose Ava and Bethany to such an argument.

"Pull yourself together and give me a call when you're ready to act like an adult." He left the house without stopping to hug his precious nieces.

The hours driving back to the city were a blur, and Lachlan did not bother stopping at either his penthouse or his office at the House. Instead, he made a swift beeline directly to his club, ordering neat scotch from the very top shelf.

CHAPTER 8 - SARA

When Lachlan left Sara burst into tears and fled into
the garden, escaping the prying eyes of her daughters.
Ava would have accepted any lame excuse she offered,
but Bethany, despite her young years, would probe
and probe, and Sara feared she would explode at them,
an unintended target of her fear and anger.
She paced the perimeter of the house gardens,
stomping across carefully plotted meandering paths
and pristine lawns, untouched by the beauty around
her. She stomped across the gravelled drive, ignoring
the calls of the girls from the house.
"Mum! Where'd you go?" Ava, the anxious older
child.
"Can we watch TV?" This from Bethany, whom Sara
new damn well already had the remote in her
mischievous hands.
Feeling like a monster she ignored them and rounded
the stables, taking long, hurried, outraged strides. She
ignored the whinnies of the four well cared for animals
in the stables, and made her way to the dam, stopping
only at the water's edge.

A few years ago, she had taken a small water storage dam left behind by the past owners and extended it, adding curving banks and areas of shallower and deeper waters. She had planted reeds and aquatic plants, as well as a backdrop of native shrubs, so that the banksias and callistemons flowered in the direction of the setting sun. It was her favourite place to think, and the tiny lake had thrived under her care. Last August, for their anniversary, Tim had toiled in the shed, an absolute woodworking rookie, but he had eventually presented her with a handcrafted bench, which they installed at the best sunset viewing vantage point. The memory of how he had joked about learning carpentry from YouTube videos designed for teenagers failed to quell her temper, but she loved that wobbly bench.

Now, she plonked on it tiredly, her body seething with too many emotions to handle right now. She closed her eyes and struggled to clear her mind. She banished the faces of Dawn, of Lachlan, of their hurt and anger at her. She shook them from her and concentrated only on the sounds around her - the low call of Banjo frogs and whine of lazy bush flies - and revelled in the feel of the soft heat of the last of the sun's rays.

She did not hear Tim's car arrive and was not sure how much time had passed when a cracking twig behind her heralded his arrival. Turning, she watched him walk toward her, his hands thrust into his chino's.

"Hi," she said over her shoulder.

Tim joined her on the bench.

"Ava said you'd be here," he said, planting a kiss atop
her head. She loved it when he kissed her head. It
always made her feel safe. Today, however, it made
her feel childish. Or perhaps it was hindsight doing
that.
"Wanna talk about it? The girls said Lachy has been
here. They said you argued."
Sara sniffed. God, she hoped she did not cry.
"Bloody kids," she said, trying to sound cheerful, but
Tim did not smile. Sara sighed.
"He came to talk me into being a team player." Tim
still did not smile, so Sara sighed again and continued.
"I just can't get past this anger Tim. I'm angry at
Lachy, and Dawn obviously. But at Dad too. And
you." She has the grace to glance apologetically at him
and he puts a hand on her knee. "I don't trust Tasmin,
and I don't see the point knowing anything about a
dead brother." She saw Tim flinch at her grim turn of
phrase, so she spoke on, hurriedly apologising for her
harsh gaff.
"Sorry. But do you see my point? We were fine until
she came along. We were all fine, despite the shitstorm
going on in the world. And yet Dawn still went
looking for this baby." She stood and scuffed the dry
ground at the water's edge. "Why? Why did she go
looking? How did she think it would turn out? Even if
he - Logan - was alive, it sounds like he was a piece of
work." Tim looked at her quizzically and reluctantly
Sara explained what Lachlan had told her. "It's just a

hunch he has," she said begrudgingly. "He could be wrong - he's blindsided by her too."

Tim looked up at his wife, framed by the setting sun, encircled by this beautiful place she had created. Quietly he spoke.

"She does have a certain fragility about her," he said "What if Lachy's hunch is correct? What if he's right and Tasmin has had a really bad time of it?"

His face was full of love as he delivered a final sentence. "Can you sleep at night if this girl has been abused, and you make it worse and turn your back on her?"

Sara did not sleep. Damn Tim and his logic, she thought crankily at 2am. Damn his kindness and his compassion and his bloody warmth for humankind. With sleep eluding her she dared to explore her true feelings. Anger? Yep, that was still there. Fear? Yep, it was there too. Suspicion? Definitely. But there was something else too, something more uncomfortable. She tossed in the king-sized bed as Tim slumbered peacefully beside her.

Sara knew she felt an anger at Dawn, a rage based on fear of the unknown, and felt justified at having that emotion. Ok, perhaps she had acted unreasonably, but fear of the unknown was hardly a crime. She was pissed at feeling excluded from the obvious bond Dawn and Lewis suddenly had, but now, in the dark quiet room, Sara realised they had always been a close, solid couple. In fact, their marriage was legendary within their social circle, and for good reason. When Lewis and Dawn proclaimed to be a team, they meant it.

This had not interfered with the special place in Lewis' heart she had always held, Sara realised, and in the silence of the night, a tiny piece of anger slipped away.

The next morning, she overslept, and when she awoke, she searched through the house, seeking out her husband. She found him outside, working on his laptop, in the morning sun.

She kissed him and enquired about the girls.

"Still sleeping," he answered, sliding a gaze sidewards to her. "It's Saturday."

"Oh," she said, stealing a sip of his coffee. "Sure. I knew that." He laughed at her then.

"Rough night?"

She nodded. "My head kept me awake."

He nodded in unison. "You were pretty restless, even when you did finally crash."

She laughed aloud, feeling lighter than she had in weeks. "And how the hell would you know, Mr Byrnes? You were asleep before your head hit the damn pillow."

He smiled indulgently. "The virtuous sleep soundly."

Sara rolled her eyes exaggeratedly and they chuckled together.

"I think," Sara said, slowly and Tim gave her his full attention. "I may have overreacted." She stared at her husband, daring him to interject, but Tim wisely chose to ignore the dangling bait.

"Go on," he said.

"I am still worried about what might happen. This girl came into our lives so quickly and she could just as quickly disappear again." She blew out a breath. "But that is not anything I have control over, and what will be, will be. I know my family loves me, and the girls, and even you." Tim grinned at this.

"I think what terrifies me most is that everything might change, and since the lockdown and everything that is going on with the VS virus, I guess I projected that by being an asshole."

Tim leaned across and kissed her fully on the mouth. Sara drank in the heat of his lips and felt an immense relief as the rage and worry seeped from her limbs. When they parted, Tim tenderly stroked her cheek.

"Go have a shower," he said. "Before the girls wake up. The only way you'll get away alone is if you manage to leave before they pester you."

CHAPTER 9 - TASMIN

As Sara tossed and turned hundreds of kilometres away, Tasmin was pulled from a deep sleep by a persistent ringing. It invaded her dreams and pulled her reluctantly towards wakefulness. Opening her eyes in the darkness she was momentarily confused until her eyes adjusted to the gloom and the now familiar apartment revealed itself in the shadows.

Fumbling to click on the bedside lamp Tasmin squinted at the sudden brightness, still feeling disorientated. What was that noise?

The metallic ringing continued until she realised it was the doorbell and she padded to the intercom beside the front door.

"Hello?" Her voice was husky with interrupted sleep.

"Tas-min? It's Lachy. Lachlan." His voice sounded strange. "Lemme in."

Confused, she pressed the button that unlocked the downstairs foyer, and then unlocked the deadbolt that secured the front door. Before long, the elevator pinged and released a rumpled Lachlan into the hallway. He staggered towards her, past her clumsily and perched on the arm on the nearest sofa.

"Hey," he said, squinting up at her.
"Are you pissed?" Tasmin could not work out what was going on; her sleep muddled mind was working so slowly.
Lachlan hiccupped. "No' really." His slurred words and slightly unfocused eyes said otherwise. Tasmin recognised their redness and smelled the tang of straight alcohol that wafted from her late-night visitor. "What do you want, Lachlan? It's late. I was asleep."
"Sorry," he said, slipping from the arm of the sofa to slouch more comfortably in the seat.
"I went to see Sara today," he began. "I jus' wanted her to see that you're no threat to her precious image. That Logan and you and the baby are not a big deal, y'know?" He was speaking rapidly and Tasmin sank into the sofa opposite. From experience she knew this energy could continue for some time.
Lachlan purged his every thought. He told her about his lonely life. He told her about his disillusionment with the Party and the way he never felt quite worthy of being Lewis' son. He spoke in disjointed sentences, jumping from one family member to another, from one topic to another, and at times Tasmin was quite lost, but her input was not really needed anyway. Lachlan appeared to have indulged in the bender to end all benders, admitting to drinking his way through the upset of being emotionally reamed by his older sister. Tasmin doubted it was only drink that had brought about this transformation in the usually elegant Senator but kept that suspicion to herself.

Once she had established that his private club was far from the cameras of prying media hacks, and he had surrendered his car keys to the barman many, many hours earlier, she relaxed.

She boiled the kettle as he continued to speak of the horrors of overflowing critical care units, his quarantine inside the House at the height of the pandemic, the models and glamazons that ruthlessly pursued him and his despair at ever making a difference. As she brewed herself a mug of herbal tea and handed him a bottle of spring water, he admitted a new anger and resentment towards his sister. Tasmin could hear the sadness in his voice as he fumbled with unfamiliar thoughts.

"I don' even know why I'm fighting with her," he slurred. "What do I care if you two don't get along. None of my business." He seemed to be winding down now. He had stopped pacing the apartment and following her around the kitchen and had returned to the sofa.

"I dunno why I give two shits. I dunno why I want you to feel like a part of this shit show." He hiccupped gracelessly. "I always try to keep out of everyone's, y'know … stuff."

Tasmin thought he looked like a sad, lost little boy, and felt a rush of tenderness for him. It rose, unbidden, in her very centre.

She tried to interject, to apologise for the mess she was making of their family, but Lachlan waved her platitudes away with a dismissive, languid swipe of this hand through the air.

He was still mumbling stuttered protestations of support for her and the child when his head finally fell forward, and he was quiet.

Tasmin remained on the sofa opposite Lachlan for long enough to believe the heavy breaths signalled deep sleep. Only then did she carefully drape his still body, and quietly pad back to her own bed, where she lay awake for a long time, staring into the darkness, more confused than ever.

CHAPTER 10 - LACHLAN

The digital sound invaded his brain, and without opening his eyes Lachlan moved his head only slightly and was rewarded with a dizzying sensation. At his temples, a headache of epic proportions thundered, banging his dehydrated brain mercilessly. His brain was not alone - his mouth and tongue were an arid wasteland, devoid of any moisture, save a tacky, sticky, useless residue of the night before.

Keeping his movements slow to avoid another wave of nausea he slowly opened one eye but quickly slammed it shut as the morning sunlight pierced his skull.

Oh, God, he thought. *This was going to be a bad one.*

He lay back, eyelids safely closed, as he did a head-to-toe assessment of the damage. No stranger to a hangover, Lachlan was today more disorientated and groggier than usual, and his body was stiff and aching. As he returned to consciousness Lachlan realised he was not in his bed, but on a narrow lounge of some kind. His back screeched in protest when he tried to roll, and his neck was still from the awkward position he had slept in.

He risked another peak into the room and despite his pupils reacting violently to the burst of light, he forced them to remain open. Blinking, he took in the airy apartment, the obviously new furniture and the wall to ceiling windows over the cityscape - they were responsible for the blinding sunlight that continued to drill its way into his cranium.

"Good morning." The words were spoken softly, and he was ridiculously grateful for the quiet tone.

Lachlan looked up and was surprised to see Tasmin standing before him, a short floral gown tied tightly across her middle, which bore the unmistakable shape of the child within.

Questions cascaded through his befuddled brain. How did he get here? Why? What had happened? How much did he drink? The effort to make sense of this day was exhausting already.

"What am I doing here?" he croaked, and as if on cue, Tasmin handed him a tall glass filled with mineral water. He accepted it and drank greedily, and though it soothed his parched mouth and throat the guzzle roiled threateningly in his alcohol molested stomach. Tasmin looked back at him. "I really have no idea. You just … arrived."

Lachlan raised himself to a sitting position, swallowing thickly as his head and stomach joined forces to protest at the movement. He closed his eyes with a long, low moan.

The buzzing, ringing jingle continued, and the noise was now joined by the sound of a door opening somewhere behind him, followed by some soft words murmured.

He trawled through his liquor-soaked brain for clues to who that soft voice could belong to. He was too far away and too ill to make out any of the words, but he heard the soft click of a door latch being released. When Sara entered the apartment, it took just a few steps before she spotted him. With one sweep of her widening eyes, she took in the scene before her. Lachlan, seated on the sofa, the clothes she recognised from yesterday rumpled and creased, his hair mussed, and Tasmin before him, in pretty, botanical print sleepwear.

"Oh. My. God." Sara spoke deliberately. "I came here to speak to you." She glared at Tasmin now. "I came to apologise and ask if we could start over again, but I see you've already slept your way into a better position I could ever offer."

Tasmin made a small noise and stepped backwards, away from Lachlan and away from the barbed sting of Sara's accusation.

"No!" she protested. "No. That's not what happened …"

"Save it," Sara spat. "I don't want to hear any excuse you have." She dismissed Tasmin without a further word, turning her anger at Lachlan.

"You are a pathetic piece of work Lachy. A bloody hopeless pain in my arse. It's not as if you couldn't find someone else to sleep with, given your past couple of years, or have you run out of conquests?"

Lachlan wished he could jump to his feet to battle his sister - seated here she towered over him - but he doubted he could without vomiting on the dove grey carpet.

"You've got this wrong," he began, but Sara allowed him little space to speak.

"Oh, have I?" she challenged. "Then please, enlighten me Senator. Tell me what's going on here."

The confusion that clouded Lachlan's face was obvious - how could he explain what had happened when he did not even know himself?

Sara sneered at him. "Just as I thought. The gold digger has targeted the weakest link, and as usual, you fell for it." She turned and stomped from the room, not bothering to close the apartment door behind her. In the silence, Lachan could hear her jabbing at the buttons on the elevator, before swearing loudly and choosing the stairs instead.

As her footsteps echoed away Lachlan remembered Tasmin standing stiffly on the other side of the room, and looked at her, embarrassment evident in his expression.

"I'm sorry," he said. "I don't quite know what just happened, but I am sorry." He rose to his feet, unsteadily at first, but with sheer will he forced his body to an upright position. "Maybe I should just go."

Tasmin looked at him, her expression unreadable. Then she said. "Don't let me keep you. By the sounds of it you have a very full schedule of women to call in on, so please, don't worry about me." He saw a flash in her eyes and realised she was close to tears. He suspected she was using all her might to keep them from falling, and he did not blame her. Sara had been far from complimentary.

"Just so you know, I didn't ask you here. You barged in at 2am, pissed and probably high, and carried on about your family and an argument with Sara and how Lewis doesn't love you enough and how so unfair your life is." She was really wound up now, Lachlan observed. Her hands were small tight balls at her side and the top of her pale breasts heaved as she spoke, more angrily now.

"I am NOT the issue here Lachlan. I have tried everything to be respectful and give you all space, but you and Sara really need to sort your own shit out. Whatever all this is..." she gestured wildly "...has little to do with me, and more to do with a couple of spoiled brats feeling threatened by the real world." Lachlan thought he may well pass out. He felt dreadful. Sara had yelled. Tasmin was still yelling, and he just wanted to disappear into a hole in the ground. *Was it possible to die from a hangover?* he wondered. Imagine the headlines. 'Senator killed by vintage scotch poisoning.'

Tasmin's voice rose again. "So, get out Lachlan. Get out and don't bother me again. I thought you were different to your sister, but you are exactly the same. A pair of asshole children who have never had to grow up, and I don't want to be around either of you."

She fell silent, and with pitiful self-loathing Lachlan took the opportunity to escape. Unlike Sara he carefully closed the door to the apartment, briefly leaning on the door jam in embarrassment, before heading downstairs and into the fresh air of the city.

It had not taken Lachlan long to hail a cab and make his way to his own penthouse apartment, where he fashioned a quick protein shake. Stripping off his slept-in clothes and leaving them where they lay, he sipped slowly in the fortifying pulse of his massaging shower. The thick drink sat uneasily in his stomach to begin with, but Lachlan persisted, and with each sip, felt marginally better. Stepping from the shower he chose not to bother with a towel, enjoying the sensation as the water droplets evaporated from his taut body, vaporising some of the misery.
He grabbed a bottle of vitamin water from the fridge and padded to his room, falling onto the bed to sleep off his headache and escape the regret of the past few hours.

The sun was low in the sky when he awoke and though he still felt sluggish and fatigued, Lachlan was ravenous with hunger. Normally his hangovers were fed with a large meal, a creamy pasta or rare steak with crispy fries. Usually, Lachlan would either meet up at some inner-city eatery with the same friends he had partied with or pick up a meal on the route home from the bed of whichever femme fatale he had cavorted

with. Very rarely did Lachlan date - he could probably
count on one hand the number of times he had asked
a woman to share a meal with him for purely social
reasons. Usually, an invitation had an ulterior motive;
Dawn was attempting to set him up with a potential
mate and he hated to disappoint her, or he needed a
date to complete a picture-perfect photo opportunity
at a Party function.

Today was different. Admittedly, he had fled a
woman's apartment earlier in the day, but under
different circumstances and he had not dared stop off
anywhere, lest he vomit on the street. As images from
the night before started to flash back to him, he could
remember very few familiar faces. It seems he had
drunk alone, save for the couple of drinks he shared
with a flashy young guy. Lachlan remembered the
man, all slick haircut and heavy chains nuzzled on his
chest, and his discreet supply of just enough cocaine
to allow Lachlan to drink even more.

What disturbed him beyond the sad picture he must
have made at the club, were the staccato memories of
the things he had told Tasmin. He remembered
weaving his way there, through the almost deserted
early morning streets, but cannot recall the decision to
do so. Each flashback from her cosy, moonlit
apartment caused him to cringe. He winced recalling
telling her about the pursuit of Lewis' approval, and
the memory of his tears when he had tried to describe
how the pandemic now flooded him with remorse.

What had possessed him to go to her? Admittedly he felt a strange protectiveness of Tasmin, an emotion that baffled him in its intensity and oddity. Lachlan knew his behaviour in the past had been selfish and self-centred, but - in his defence - no one had ever minded, and it helped him keep everyone at an arm's length. There was no chance of being hurt, if you did not allow yourself to care, he reasoned.

Unbidden, an image of Kate flashed through his mind and his heart lurched in response. Enough time had passed for Lachlan to concede he loved her. *Had loved her*, he corrected. Their relationship had been more than inappropriate, and it was fortunate they had narrowly escaped causing lasting harm to her marriage and children. As much as he missed her, Lachlan wondered, in hindsight, whether he missed Kate herself, or the warmth a relationship offered. Perhaps it was both.

Listlessly Lachlan browsed the cupboards of his sleek modern kitchen and found little to tempt his taste buds. The fridge was similarly disappointing, and on a whim, he threw on some track pants and a faded tee from a music festival held long ago, grabbed his keys, and headed out of the penthouse. As he descended, he wondered if crowded music festivals would ever be possible again.

Along the street from his home a small avenue of shops had been established under a neighbouring block of expensive units. There was an Italian delicatessen, an organic bakery, a small butcher, and a café, manned by bearded young men in denim and leather aprons.

Lachlan rarely used the shops, preferring to eat out, either with colleagues and friends, or at various functions across the city. Even during lockdown, he had not shopped for groceries, relying instead on the House of Parliament catering services, or the food parcels delivered from Marg's own kitchen. He could not remember the last time he had done more than reheat a meal.

He stopped at the butcher first, selecting a plump chicken breast, and two narrow slivers of cured bacon. At the deli he chose a jar of sun-dried tomatoes, swimming in imported olive oil, some fresh asparagus, and a small jar of rich cream. Hovering in front of an assortment of fresh pasta he decided on orecchiette, before throwing some staples into his shopping basket. He bought a small brick of spiced fruit loaf at the bakery, then settled at an outdoor table and waited until a denim clad hipster delivered him a piping hot mug of coffee. He sipped at it carefully while he watched the handful of people going about their business in front of him. The coffee was good, and it helped ease the faint drumbeat of headache that still echoed in his temples.

Across the road a car eased into a space, and a man about Lachlan's age stepped out of the driver's seat. He quickly moved to the back of the car and Lachlan watched him expertly remove a pram, and with a few flicks, had it expertly unfolded and safely on the footpath. A woman joined him, softly murmuring into a bundle of blankets, before she gently laid a baby into the pram. The man put his arm around the woman's shoulders and Lachlan watched as she leant back into his body when he kissed the top of her head. Together they pushed the pram up the street and away from him, and Lachan felt an unfamiliar, but unmistakable, pang of envy.

Christ, this hangover was messing him up. He finished his coffee, left a large tip for the waiter, and lugged his groceries the short distance home.

Later, having searched Google for a fool proof recipe, he sat in front of a rugby league grand final replay, balancing a huge bowl of creamy chicken pasta on his knees. It was too hot, but he gobbled it hungrily anyway, feeling healthier with every bite. It tasted better than anything he had eaten in recent memory, he thought, and sent up a silent apology to Marg, suburbs away. If only she could see him now, he thought, and a small, proud smile played on his lips.

Lachlan coped with the emotional upheaval and unusual lack of confidence the only way he knew how. The next weeks passed in a blur of work and alcohol, as he threw himself into anything and everything, in order to fill every moment of each day.

He was at his desk before most of his staff, pouring through the enormous amount of reading required. In the past he had allocated many tasks to staffers and Party volunteers, who read each long, dry report or

medical paper with dedication, and presented him with
a succinct one-page summary, that he then used to
appear informed and up to date. Now, he poured over
each word himself, making notes on a scribble pad
that Harry the PA deftly typed and filed according to
subject, department, and date. His staff quickly
adapted to his new workflow, organising themselves to
ensure his office was staffed almost around the clock,
but Lachlan barely noticed. He moved through his
days as if he were wearing mental blinkers; he only
allowed his mind to concentrate on matters of national
importance. Nothing personal. Nothing family related.
And nothing Tasmin flavoured.

When he was not at the House, he used his luxurious
apartment only to shower and change, and perhaps
catch a few hours sleep. He avoided his own home,
lest he allow himself to relax and his mind to wander.
It was a similar pattern of behaviour that had saved
him when Kate unceremoniously exited his life, but
this time it felt much harder to keep his mind away
from delicate subjects. Lachlan was exhausted with the
effort it took to keep his head from examining his
heart.

His drinking buddies welcomed him with open arms.
Colleagues and ex-classmates with their own reasons
to avoid home shared copious amounts of top shelf
liquor and bottom of the barrel conversations. Each
refused to discuss anything resembling a meaningful
conversation and Lachlan was grateful for their

shallowness. He too, was emotionally shallow to the point of emptiness.

Women approached him and he eyed them coolly through a drunken filter but took none of them up on their offers. Scantily clad breasts. Long, shapely legs pressed against his. Blatant come-on lines that would have made a sailor blush. None of it moved him, and his cronies noticed. They ribbed and joked, making fun of the legendary Wolfe turning down offers of uncomplicated sex without the blink of an eye. Lachlan learned to silence their amusement by ordering a round of drinks, or discretely motioning to their favourite barman that a small amount of cocaine should be arranged.

His life was hollow, devoid of any real friends, but this crowd was exactly what he needed until his heart hardened again.

He ignored Sunday dinners with his family and had Harry shoot off impersonal emails to Dawn and Sara when they attempted contact. From Tasmin he heard nothing.

CHAPTER 11 - LACHLAN

Lachlan could hear a loud conversation outside his office, which was unusual. Usually, his heavy door muffled all sounds when he closed it for privacy, and his staff had been exceptionally quiet lately; what he failed to see was everyone treating him carefully and walking on eggshells to avoid his blunt, caustic manner.

He returned to his work, but Harry's raised voice interrupted his flow of thought once again.

"Mr Byrnes! I must insist. Senator Wolfe has closed off his calendar to guests right now, and I …" Harry's platitudes quickly became redundant as Tim opened the door and beamed at him cheerfully, Lachlan scowled, first at Tim, who ignored his obvious bad temper, and then at Harry who cowled in the doorway.

"Get out," he told a nervous Harry, who left without word, closing the door behind him.

Sitting back Lachlan coolly watched his brother-in-law take a seat in the plush armchair to one side of the room, ignoring the equally opulent but less comfortable desk chair opposite the Senator's desk.

"I'm busy Tim." Even Lachan could hear the weariness in his voice. "What do you want?" It was blunt. But Lachlan could not help it. He liked Tim, loved him as a brother he had never had - *or known about*, he thought - but he seemed unable to inject any warmth into his tone these days.

"I don't give a shit how busy you are, mate," Tim answered pleasantly. "You've ignored every call, every email. You don't come to Dawn's for lunch anymore and you have had your minions out there refuse entry to your own damn mother." Tim indicated the outer office with a gesture of his head, and Lachlan felt a smidgen of shame as he remembered giving the directive not to admit Dawn. He said nothing though, so Tim continued.

"I have always admired you Lachy." *Have you?* Lachlan wanted to ask and was surprised at the rush of emotion Tim's words evoked. "But you are acting like a tool right now. I understand you probably feel torn between everyone right now, and God knows I have tried to get Sara to see reason." Lachlan could see the frustration etched on Tim's face.

"But we're worried about you Lach. Actually, fuck everyone else. Fuck you Wolfe's - *I'm* worried about you buddy. Really worried." Lachlan saw the concern in Tim's eyes and felt his anger slowly deflating. Slowly, like a sagging helium balloon leftover from a wild twenty-first party.

"Talk to me mate," Tim implored softly.

Where could he start?

In short, faltering sentences Lachlan tried to unpack exactly what was going on. He trusted Tim, but he struggled to find the words. Oh, the irony! He was paid well for his debate skills and his conversation expertise had seen him easily elected, but now he floundered in the face of such concern.

Lachlan started by telling Tim how much easier it was to avoid the family, than be thrust into the role of mediator of that toxic combat each visit. He spoke about his shame at his behaviour at Tasmin's apartment and how he felt helpless to ease Sara's anger. He talked about feeling like he never met Lewis' expectations, no matter how successful his career, and how he felt sorry for Dawn, having all this thrown up right now. The more he spoke, the easier the words seemed to spill from him.

He spoke of the disconcerting confusion as a previously unseen ugly side to Sara's personality emerged and noted Tim's little chuckle. He even admitted feeling ashamed of his playboy past, seeing it now from Tasmin's point of view. Until now, a reputation as a lady killer and womaniser was part of his role, an expectation almost forced upon him, in the male dominated Party and his own social circle.

Tim was silent for most of this, offering a nod here or a quiet prompt there, allowing Lachlan to finally get a lot of his complex emotions out into the open.

Lachlan had no idea how much time had passed. He had paced the room, finding it easier not to face Tim as he spoke, but now, spent, he dropped onto the sofa, beside Tim. God he was tired.

"You know what I think?" Tim posed a question and Lachlan was not sure he wanted to know. He grunted instead, not game to actually ask his friend's opinion. "You are avoiding all of us as a way of avoiding yourself. You are a great guy Lachlan, and I have always thought the partying and sleeping around was just a way you dealt with loneliness." *Ouch*, Lachlan thought, but Tim was not finished.

"You are one of the most talented and driven men I know, but even though you come across all confident and sure of yourself, you have a lot of hesitation about you. You are so aware of Lewis and failing whatever it is you think he expects of you, that you don't actually do anything." Tim gestured around the office. "What are you hoping to achieve here Lach? As a Senator? What is it you want to do? Because if you don't have a burning desire to be here and make a change, you should move aside for someone who does." His voice was kind, but the words stabbed at Lachlan.

"So you think I'm useless too? Gee, thanks Tim." Lachlan's childish voice betrayed the hurt he was feeling, but he could not help it.

Tim shook his head. "Nah mate, but there you go again. You are immediately defensive instead of really listening to what I have said. I don't think you're useless, but I do think you haven't reached your potential yet." He stood up, and Lachlan was sad to realise their conversation was coming to an end.

"You have too much natural ambition to not do great things, either as a Senator or as Lachy Wolfe," Tim continued. "But you are an absolute master at trying to avoid your problems by ignoring them and everyone around you, and from here it looks like it's eating you up. You look like shit mate, and everyone out there in that office is scurrying around terrified, because your mood is so damn foul." Tim sighed. "Look, you are a grown man, but I suggest you ring your bloody parents and email your sister. And apologise to Tasmin for arriving at her place in the middle of the night like a drunk teenager. Get some new friends and try and work out what it is you want from your life." During this monologue Lachlan had remained on the sofa, but Tim had moved across the room and now stood with his hand on the doorknob.

"Maybe send these poor bastards home early too," he said with a grin, pointing towards the outer office. "I bet they deserve it."

Lachlan returned the smile, wryly, but it felt natural and good to be experiencing any emotion other than shame and annoyance. "Point taken," he replied, and Tim slipped from the room.

Lachlan remained in place, his head spinning from the truths uncovered during Tim's visit. The empty life he had described was mortifying, as was his behaviour towards his family. And Tasmin - what must she think of him? No wonder she had turfed him from her home. Her life had been through such an upheaval in the past months, and then along he came to make it even worse. He could only imagine what she had been through, but he had learned enough over their long lunch at Vito's too many weeks ago to know her life had been fraught.

He remembered how flat her words had been when she spoke of Logan, his brother, and thought back to how she described the impact of the lockdown on them. The pandemic and the widespread loss of work seemed to have been a turning point of some kind, and Lachlan felt a spark of an idea form in his mind. Perhaps…

Striding to the door he flung it open and was dismayed at the startled expressions on the faces of his team. A couple of the younger employees appeared downright fearful.

He cleared his throat and plunged right in. "I apologise for my behaviour over the last couple of weeks," he said. "It won't happen again." With a few curt instructions he directed them all to finish up for the day and head home. He set up a staff meeting for 9am the following morning and disappeared back into his office, this time leaving the door open.

"And I don't want to see anyone in here before the meeting tomorrow," he said over his shoulder, and was pleased at the murmurs of delight behind him. Lachlan worked through the night. He searched through pilot program guidelines and researched articles online. He trawled through his own Party's projects and those of counterparts around the world. He could not find anything that suited his purpose exactly, but he began to form a clear outline of a project, as he scribbled notes on the whiteboard and pounded away at his keyboard.

He ordered food, which was delivered to him by the security guard, and he showered and changed clothes when his energy lagged. He snatched a couple of power naps on the thick carpet of his office, but as dawn broke, he felt more energised and alive than ever. The program proposal in front of him needed work but he knew it was good. He knew, perhaps for the first time in his career, that he had something tangible that could really help change people's lives. When his staff began to arrive the next day he assembled them in the office, his notes now contained in a neat pile, and the whiteboard scribbles replaced with more legible text. He handed around steaming mugs, having taken the time to put in a customised order from the favourite coffee shop around the corner, who kept meticulous records of staff preferences. He noted the pleasure his small gesture made and was even more buoyed by the pleasure this small act gave him. He also noted the surprise on everyone's faces, when he greeted them in a tight tee, baggy basketball shorts and runners, his only options once he had showered in the early hours of the morning. He did not care about the clothes he was wearing. For once, his carefully cultivated image was far from his mind.

He asked everyone for their attention and began to outline his plan, and their part in it.

CHAPTER 12 - LEWIS

"Lewis Wolfe speaking." Lewis' voice was gruff. He was reading over the latest financial report, showing an increase in his business wealth despite the economic downturn, but the positive report offered no challenge. If Lewis was honest, he was bored.
It seemed insensitive to admit boredom for such a charmed life, but even though he was rich and powerful, Lewis was a worker at heart. A problem solver. He knew he was often painted as ruthless, and while the perception did not bother him, it was not entirely true. What drove him was taking an unprofitable business and turning it into an efficient enterprise that employed people and returned a dividend to investors. If that was ruthlessness, then Lewis had learned to live with the character trademark.
"Lewis it's me. It's Lachlan." His son's voice down the phone line sounded different somehow, almost eager. Lewis had given Lachlan space after the disastrous incident at Tasmin's home that night. As a father he had been incensed at Lachlan's behaviour, and Sara's rude rage, and had developed even more protectiveness over Tasmin. He and Dawn had spent a

fair amount of time with the girl, getting to know her better and quietly ignoring their other children as they grappled with this unexpected knowledge of a new family member.

Tasmin gently refused their invitations to Sunday lunch, and Lachlan's abrupt absence had left them to enjoy a visit with their cherished granddaughters each week instead. And their parents, Lewis ruefully added. Sara's reaction to Tasmin had cut him to his soul. He loved his daughter, as any father should, but he also openly admired her. He respected her drive and ambition and marvelled at the way she courted success, but he had never known her act with such cruelty. To Dawn - her own mother - and to young Tasmin. That shook Lewis, and as he heard his son's voice he wondered if Lachlan was also struggling to cope with this newly discovered spitefulness in the woman they both adored.

"Lachlan. What a nice surprise." He leaned back in his chair, cradling the receiver against his shoulder, as he reached for the mug of dark tea he had not yet tasted. There was a pause at the end of the line; had his greeting startled his son, Lewis wondered. But it was the truth. He had missed seeing Lachlan, debating issues with him, and having an insight into the workings of the Government.

"I have a proposal I wish to run past you Lewis," Lachlan finally said, and Lewis tried to ignore the familiar disappointment when his son called him by his first name.

"I'm listening," Lewis said, and he was. As he sipped at the tea, he mused that he could not recall a time Lachlan had come to him with any sort of project - even his political career had evolved from a suggestion by a dear old friend of Lewis'. Lachlan had simply agreed.

He heard Lachlan take a deep breath. "I want us to set up a charity," he said. "I want the Wolfe Foundation to branch out and set up a not-for-profit organisation, in response to the pandemic." He paused, and Lewis could hear his rapid breathing. Lachlan pushed on. "The Department of Health is having issues rolling out the vaccine. We simply don't have enough medical staff available in the country - most are still working in intensive care, and we don't have time to wait for the next batch of Uni graduates. The vaccine needs to roll out now." Lewis could hear the passion in his voice and felt a surge of pride. It was good to hear Lachlan sound so enthused.

"Go on," he prompted.

"We have the stocks. Production is not the issue; it's getting the vaccine hubs set up and getting the logistics right." He suddenly changed tack, momentarily confusing Lewis.

"Apart from the death toll, what is the next major issue the country is facing right now?" Lachlan asked.

"Well … I would have to say unemployment," Lewis replied. "And the issues that it is causing for those of us who still have work to do. You should hear the old boys at my club grumbling about tax hikes to cover welfare payments." Lachlan let out a short laugh and Lewis supposed calling others 'old' was a bit funny. He was old himself, but he hated to admit it.

"That's it," Lachlan said. "Without work for people to do, we are going to be dealing with a lot more than just Government debts. Something Tasmin said to me has been playing on my mind." Lewis could sense his son was pacing as they spoke, a habit he recalled from his own highly-strung younger days.

"Tasmin told me when Logan lost his job, it caused some sort of problem between them, and can you imagine what it must have been like for people to suddenly be without work, on welfare for the first time, feeling useless and scared?" Lachlan did not give Lewis time to answer.

"If we can't turn the unemployment rate around and get people working, then we are going to be dealing with a lot of long-term social issues for decades, and that is where it will get expensive for the Government." He scoffed. "The old blokes have no idea of the magnitude of tax we will need to raise in the future to support a traumatised, bored community, with no self-worth." Lachlan took another breath and Lewis realised he was nervous. *About speaking to me? Oh no, surely not.*

"You have my full attention Lachlan," he said encouragingly. "What's your proposal?"

He heard Lachlan's audible gulp.

"What if we could combine the two issues? My team has done a lot of work in the past week, and I will email you the full briefing paper, but before I go to the Party, I need to know you are with me on this."

Lewis did not need to consider it. Just moments ago, he had been tired and disinterested in his business, and now here was Lachlan - his son - coming to him with a challenge that mattered.

"I'm in. Whatever it is, I'm in. Tell me more."

The pair talked on the phone for more than an hour. Lachlan emailed Lewis the document his team had prepared, and they poured over each statistic, budget item and paragraph. They were physically miles apart, yet Lewis had never felt closer to his son.

He thought Lachlan's plan was brilliant and told him so. It brought a smile to his face to hear the joy and pride in Lachlan's voice when he accepted the compliment.

Lachlan's proposal outlined the dollar terms cost of supporting a nation of long-term unemployed people, coupled with the United Nations' predictions of the costs of recovering from the pandemic. It cited projections on the increase in domestic violence and the strain on community service agencies, and it touted the impact on children and their futures. Lewis thought this was a clever inclusion; after all, children are future taxpayers, and voters.

The idea itself was simple. Train those who had lost their jobs due to the virus to undertake the administrative tasks required to set-up and man the vaccine hubs and use their local knowledge to site the hubs in the best places, to reach people quickly. Those with existing medical qualifications - nurses, doctors, virologists - would then be freed up to undertake the supervision of a team and get the vaccine into the arms of those desperate for it.

The crux of the proposal was the commitment of the Wolfe families newly established charity to fund the training and recruitment costs, nationwide.

When Lachlan threw out a projected figure cost Lewis let out a low whistle. It was a huge commitment, no doubt, but he could think of nothing more he wanted to spend his money on.

"Let's get it started Lachlan," he said stretching his aching back. The marathon session had begun to wear on his bones, but his mind exploded with the possibilities the program could offer.

"There's just one last thing we need to decide," Lachlan said, and Lewis was surprised. What had he forgotten? They had already decided on several wonderful people to approach with a Board position and tidied up some wording in the draft proposal.

"I'd like to name the charity, if that's ok with you," Lachlan paused. "I think it should be called the Lewis Wolfe Foundation."

Lewis was speechless. He could not remember a time he had felt more humbled.

"But this is your concept, your amazing idea," he protested. "The Trust should be named for you, or the family as a whole."

Lachlan interrupted. "No, Dad. Sara and I will carry on your business, you know that, but this would not

be possible without the hard work you have put in your whole life. This is your legacy, no one else's."
Lewis hurriedly accepted, agreed to run through a final draft of the briefing paper later that day, and stabbed at the phone to disconnect the call. His eyes itched with unshed tears, and as he rose, he felt a sob escape him.
He needed to find Dawn. He had so much to tell her.

CHAPTER 13 - LACHLAN

With a dry throat Lachlan sat, nervously returning to his place in the Party room, where he had assembled various senior members of the Government, and talked endlessly about the Wolfe Proposal, as he and his staff had taken to calling it.

Together with Lewis and some of the country's most respected business denizens, Lachlan and his team had toiled over the presentation, capturing comments from community workers and doctors, and projecting them onto the large screen at one end of the room. The final moments they had dedicated to a tearful plea from a grandfather, once owner of a series of cafes, now unemployed and tasked with raising twin grandsons, the only remaining members of his once large family. The room had been hushed and Lachlan prayed the hardened hearts of the sombre crowd had at least softened at the raw emotion the man unashamedly shared.

As the lights rose Lachlan dared a glance around the room and was heartened by what he saw. Often disinterest was the flavour of the day in this room, regardless of the topic, but now he saw something else

- could it be intrigue or a caution support? And some members even appeared to be struggling to regain a stony composure, Lachlan realised. He sent a silent thank you to Harry for his suggestion to include real life, unscripted stories, and clamped down an excited smile. It was an unwritten rule in here; do not give anything away. It was ridiculously hard to keep a poker face, however, when he wanted to gush about this project so badly.

It had only taken a fortnight of hard slog to pull together the presentation, finalise the budget and find a date and time that the Party could meet. The speed spun Lachan's head but filled his heart - this was the kind of work he wanted to do, he realised, and now - finally - he had a purpose.

Lachlan could stand the silence in the room no longer. The shuffling bodies told him everyone was waiting for someone else to speak, so he decided to take charge, despite his lack of seniority among the much older, much more experienced politicians.

"Any questions?" He hoped he sounded confident. He was confident, he reminded himself. This proposal was good - it made the Government look good, it had brought him closer to his father than he had ever imagined, and together they had slaved over and built a win-win proposal for all.

Most heads swivelled towards Jonathon Carter, deputy Prime Minister and the man everyone expected to challenge Prime Minister Bonner once the nation had stabilised. The room held its collective breath as they waited to see his reaction. Lachlan admired him in a generic way, as one does for a matronly aunt or foreign diplomat, but as he waited Lachlan realised, he did not like the senior Minister. Not one bit. Carter was everything Lachlan had once felt he needed to be - powerful, ambitious, ruthless - but now, the unkind glint in the older man's eye was clear, even from across the large wood panelled room.

"Aren't you a dark horse, Senator," Carter drawled. He remained seated, leaning back in his chair as if the presentation had meant little, but Lachlan thought he could see interest in his expression.

"I have to admit, I supported your election campaign for the Wolfe name, and as a favour to a few mates, but you may have come up with something almost worthwhile here."

The jibe was cruel - deliberately cruel. Carter preferred to keep young pups in their place. Lachlan was stung by the words. He knew his success was partly because of his family and background, but surely he meant more than that? Surely he was more than just a pretty face? The knowledge that senior officials saw him as irrelevant stabbed at his insides.

This proposal must work, Lachlan thought to himself, careful to keep his face from betraying any wild emotions he was feeling. I need to prove I am worthy of this place in the Senate. I need to show I am worthy, full stop.

"But it has some merit, and I am happy to take this to the PM for you," he continued, in a deliberately off-handed manner, and Lachlan intuitively knew he may need to give up credit for this project to this bigger ego for it to succeed. He felt a familiar flash of hot anger at the unfairness, but just as quickly the heat left him. He really, truly, did not care who took the credit, as long as the project went ahead. The realisation surprised him for a moment, but he let that go too. He had learned so much about himself in these past weeks that new emotions were becoming more commonplace.

"I think it's brilliant," Every head in the room turned to a quietly spoken, pale young man, a surprise election winner, some rural electorate, Lachlan thought, but he doubted they had ever spoken two words together before today. As if alarmed by his own comments the man quickly filled the silence, delivering a rapid summary of the proposal and the benefits he could see for small towns and isolated areas. Lachlan saw he was referring to pages of cramped notes and when the man finally fell silent, Lachlan thanked him with genuine warmth. The young Senator blushed and appeared a little dazed at his own audacity.

The comments opened a floodgate of congratulations and discussion around the room, mainly positive. Some threw some curve-ball questions, but Lachlan felt he answered them all with knowledge - he knew this proposal and the economics behind it inside out. The next hour was spent in deep conversation with his colleagues, and even though Carter did not add anything further, Lachlan knew he had taken it all in.

He would no doubt re-package this and present to the
Prime Minister as his own work, but it did not matter.
All that mattered was the proposal roll out quickly,
and his father's involvement be recognised.
To himself Lachlan chuckled. Oh, how he had
changed.

Still on a high from his exhilarating day, Lachlan let
himself into his parent's mansion and burst into the
kitchen to greet Marg. There, propped at the long
marble-topped kitchen bench was Tasmin, and the
sight of her momentarily slowed him.
Her hair was longer, and it hung down her back in
loose waves the colour of a summer sunset. She wore
an emerald green top made of some sort of soft
material, that hugged her breasts and draped over her
tight ball of stomach, much larger than when he had
last seen her. He cringed internally at that memory.
She was pale but smiling and he had obviously
interrupted a chat between the two women. When she
saw him, two pink spots blushed her cheeks, but she
held his gaze, her blue eyes searching his.
"Hello," Lachlan said. "Hi. Hi you two." His voice
sounded idiotic, but he had not expected to see
Tasmin in his childhood home, sitting at the same
kitchen counter he had as a teenager. He felt off-
balance somehow.
Marg came to his rescue. "Hello yourself," she said,
crossing to peck him on the cheek. "We were just
discussing Tasmin's birthday."

He looked across the wide bench. "Birthday? Is it today? I'm sorry. I, ah, didn't know."

Tasmin smiled at him. "It's ok. I asked Dawn to keep it to herself." She shrugged gracefully, despite the round weight of the baby in her lap.

Marg looked at him and laughed. "And because of that, we're all here for dinner and cake."

As if on cue a buzzer sounded and Marg removed a high chocolate cake from the oven, its sweet, rich aroma filling the kitchen.

Bloody Dawn, Lachlan cursed. She should have told him, instead of just texting a quick "Come for dinner tonight." He would have a go at her later, he decided. "Well," he cleared his throat. "I'm sorry I didn't know. I'd have got you a gift." It was the truth. He would have enjoyed shopping for something to give her. *That's new,* his internal monologue mocked.

"Tut, tut," Marg was mocking him now too. "You'll just have to ice this monster mud cake instead. To make up for the fact you didn't bring a present." She laughed aloud at the panic that spread across his face, and Tasmin joined her. Her laugh was light, like a tinkle from a wind chime swaying in the breeze.

"I've never iced a bloody cake," he exclaimed, then grinned at Tasmin. If she was going to ignore the ass he had been last time they were together, then he could ice a damn cake to say sorry. "Show me the way," he demanded, brandishing a tea towel at Marg.

Dinner was wonderful. Lachlan realised he was having a relaxing, enjoyable meal at his parents' house, for the first time in many years. They ate at the round tiled table in the sunny room off the kitchen, ignoring the dining room and its formal place settings. Tasmin's friend Fairy and Marg joined them, and the meal was delicious - pomegranate chicken and lightly roasted new potatoes, unearthed that morning from the Wolfe's own kitchen garden.

The conversation was not forced and without the weight of Sara's continuing displeasure, everyone was enjoying the laid-back evening. Fairy held court with raucous stories from her past, and Lewis and Lachlan updated the rest of them on the progress of the Trust. Lachlan revelled in the pride that shone in Dawn and Marg's eyes and was suitably gracious when Fairy delivered one of her highest forms of praise. "You aren't as big a wanker as I first thought."

Lachlan helped Marg clear the dishes from the table and when she lifted the heavy cake from the fridge, she handed it to him.

"I think you are the best person to deliver this," she said. The smile on her face puzzled him.

"Is that because you don't want to be associated with my handiwork?" he asked, and they both giggled. Decorating the cake had taken an hour and many online tutorials, because he had foolishly ushered Marg and Tasmin from the kitchen and insisted on doing it all himself. The result was a lot of leftover chocolate frosting, many drips on the serving plate until he got the consistency right, and fresh flowers from the garden to hide some damage on one side.

Marg touched a lit match to the single candle and together they walked carefully back to the table, where Tasmin sat.

They offered her a bad rendition of the birthday song, at which she clapped delightedly, and then she cut thick wedges which were passed around the table. Silence fell as everyone devoured a week's worth of calories.

Fairy groaned as the last mouthful disappeared from her dessert fork. "I am full to the pussy's bow," she declared, and Lewis gave a shout of laughter.

"I haven't heard that saying for years!" The two beamed at each other. Now that the push-pull over Tasmin's affection had lessened the trio of Fairy, Dawn and Lewis had relaxed into an unusual but close friendship. If only Sara could relax, Lachlan though. She does not know what she is missing.

As he looked at Tasmin she inhaled sharply, and moved in her seat, placing a hand on the top swell of her stomach.

"You ok?" he asked quickly, but Tasmin smiled.

"All good," she said, a little breathlessly. "We are running out of room in here," she initiated her stomach. "I think too much cake has woken up bub, and every time it stretches now, I get a foot in the ribs."

Dawn watched her sympathetically. "You poor thing. I remember when I was pregnant with Lachlan - I swear

he did somersaults every night, just to keep me awake.
Do you remember Lewis?"
Lewis rolled his eyes dramatically. "How could I
forget? I was the one in the spare room, remember."
Lachlan had not heard this story before. "Just me?" he
asked. "Or all of us? Is it a normal thing?" In his hurry
to ensure Tasmin's discomfort was not unusual he did
not even notice he had naturally included Logan Pell
in Dawn's pregnancies.
Dawn was thoughtful. "Sara was relatively peaceful,
but then she was the smallest of you all." She paused,
but then spoke on. "Logan was the largest born,
almost nine pounds, but I don't remember much of
the pregnancy itself." Her volume dropped. "I think I
must have blocked a lot of it out, and now that I want
to remember, I can't." Lewis put a protective hand
over hers.
Lachlan noticed both Fairy and Marg were quiet, and
he wondered at their own stories of childlessness.
"Would you like to feel the baby?" Lachlan realised
Tasmin's question was directed at him, and his heart
thudded. Did he? I mean, he wanted to see what it felt
like, given the way Tasmin's top shivered over the
movement, but should he?
"Um…" His grasp on language was really escaping
him tonight.
"Go on," Fairy urged. "It's bloody incredible."
Tasmin was seated across the round table from him,
so Lachlan wiped chocolatey crumbs from his fingers
on a napkin and moved around to where she sat. She

laboriously moved around in her seat so when he knelt beside her, he faced the roundness of the child. He lifted one hand, but hesitated, no sure what to do next. Tasmin took his hand in her cool one and gently placed it on her stomach. Immediately the child kicked out at the weight of him, and Lachlan visibly jumped. The elders around the table laughed at him.

"See what I mean?" Dawn said.

Lachlan was entranced. He placed his hand on Tasmin's stomach once more and felt the child's rolling movements beneath the thinly stretched skin.

"Does it hurt?" he asked, hesitant to declare his ignorance, but wanting to know even more.

"It doesn't hurt," Tasmin replied. "It's more uncomfortable, you know? And if it's in the wrong position, up here under my ribs, it can be hard to breathe properly." He must have looked shocked because she laughed. "It's ok. It's just how the last few weeks are, apparently."

Lachlan grudgingly returned to his seat. He did not want to make a scene, but he could quite easily have stayed there, with his large hands cupping the child as it moved, but he could not quite understand why. He loved his nieces to pieces and had marvelled at their tiny perfection when they were born, but he had never before realised the power of pregnancy. Sara and he were close, but she was not the type to offer belly pats, and none of his social circle discussed children in any terms other than an inconvenience.

After Fairy and Tasmin left, and Marg and Dawn retreated, Lachlan and Lewis discussed the project for a while longer, over a pair of short black espressos. After a pause in their conversation Lewis spoke as he gazed out the window, across the darkened garden.

"Have you spoken to Sara?" he asked.

Lachlan offered a narrow shake of his head, and Lewis sighed.

"I've seen Tim, but Sara isn't responding to anything right now," Lachlan said. He toyed with the small mug in his hands, swirling the dark liquid as they broached this difficult subject.

"I know how much you love Sara," Lewis started to argue but Lachlan silenced him with a raised hand. "Honestly, Dad, it's ok. I'm not trying to fight about it, but I know how much you must be hating all this. How much you must be missing her." Lewis inclined his head wearily in agreement.

Lachlan continued, choosing his words carefully. "I love Sar too, but I am not going to chase her anymore. Now I mean no disrespect, and my own behaviour has been …" What word would suffice? he wondered. Jerk? Asshole? Brat? "… unforgivable, but I realise now that my reaction is not fair to Tasmin, or you and mum." He leaned back, holding Lewis's gaze. "But Sara refuses to conceded any of this stupid bloody reaction is her own fault. Her own jealousy. And I am sorry Dad, but until then, she is on her own. I'm not going to be her kicking boy anymore." He waited for his father's reaction.

"Good," said Lewis, surprising him.

Lachlan fell asleep almost as soon as he had stripped off and hit the cool clean sheets. The room was dark, but he had swept open the blinds and the city lights twinkled across him, as he sprawled across the massive bed.

He dreamt endlessly, and the dreams were full of Tasmin, her hair streaming out behind her as they walked through a forest full of tall trees. Her arms wrapped around a child in a blanket but as he leant forward to see the baby, she laughed and skipped away from him. He dreamt of Tasmin walking beside the ocean, outstretching a hand to his, then dragging him into the sun-drenched waves. He dreamt of her wrapping her arms around his neck in the warm, shallow waters, and pulling his lips to hers, and the taste of salt as they kissed.

He dreamt of Sara driving angrily past them on a dusty road lined with gum trees, as he and Tasmin walked hand in hand, but instead of feeling rage at his sister, the Lachlan of his dreams simply smiled and waved at the departing car.

His slumber was full of images of pushing children in swings, higher and higher as they squealed in delight, but none of the children were his nieces.

When he woke in early the next morning he was rested and calm and filled with a new knowledge. He cared for Tasmin, deeply cared for her, and the child, in a way he had not ever experienced before. He found her beautiful, of course, because she was, but he felt more than a mere, fleeting attraction for her. Although he would love nothing more right now than to kiss her soft mouth, as he had in his dream, he admitted to himself.

The whole thing was bizarre to him, but the ache he felt for her was also new, and exciting and felt so right, despite it all probably being so very wrong.

He listed off the arguments in his head, as he stretched his long, lean body in the dawn sunlight that streamed through the uncovered windows.

He hardly knew Tasmin.

She was pregnant with his dead brother's child.

Sara hated her.

He could have eligible, suitable women lined up around the block if he wanted.

But the sad truth was he just did not want any other woman. He wanted Tasmin.

Is this what love felt like? How the hell did this happen?

CHAPTER 14 - TASMIN

Across the city Tasmin was also awake, but she was feeling far from rested. The child felt like it was pummelling her from the inside out, and the last few weeks of pregnancy stretched in front of her, like a mountain to be conquered. She did not know if she had the endurance. The days seemed to be passing too slowly for her tired, overstretched body and she wished she could magically fast forward the next four weeks to her due date.

As uncomfortable as her body was, it was her the constant chatter of her mind that exhausted her the most. The previous twelve months seemed to have taken years to wade through. There was Logan's violence and death, and her own hand in that, then the discovery of Dawn and the move to the apartment. The realisation of her pregnancy had terrified her at first, but she had bloomed as the child grew and made itself known to her. Most of the time she loved the feel of the child inside her as it stretched and turned, and the love she felt already filled her tender, damaged heart with peace.

Except when that wriggling movement wakes me up too early, she thought grumpily. Her back hurt and she was sick of feeling like an uncoordinated, over-inflated balloon. But she was glad for one thing; all these bodily challenges and constant tiredness kept her mind from wandering to Lachlan.

Tasmin felt she should pinch herself on a daily basis. It seemed that one minute she had been a battered, bruised shadow of herself, living day-to-day, and the next she was safe in this beautiful apartment, with a future that glowed in front of her.

Would any of this be possible if they knew? The nagging voice inside her made her headache with guilt. Not at Logan's death, not exactly, because she knew that it had been a matter of him or me. Him or us, she thought, rubbing a hand over her stomach, where a knee or elbow protruded.

But when she thought about Dawn's reaction, she was filled with a sad, gut tightening terror. She could leave the apartment and the cocoon of financial security behind and return to Fairy's home without hesitation, but she had grown to love Dawn and Lewis. She would give all that up if she could spare Dawn any more heartache, and how would Dawn feel if she knew her firstborn had been killed by the very woman she had welcomed with so much love? Everything Sara had feared would be true.

And beyond the fear of hurting Dawn, was the dread of Lachlan knowing what she had done, what kind of person she really was. When they were together, she forgot it all, and within moments he had distracted her, and caused her to dare to dream for more. More than she ever deserved.

She had not expected to feel this gentle, soft attraction to Lachlan. She had not ever expected to feel attracted to anyone ever again, after enduring the abuse and assault Logan had dished out, in their home and their bed. Even as her body had healed under Fairy's care, it seemed her mauled soul remained damaged. She knew instantly that she could love her child, but another man? That seemed impossible.

But somehow Lachlan was under her skin. He was egotistical and spoiled and she doubted he had ever had to try hard in his entire life, and yet he intrigued her. His ego seemed forced, as if he were hiding the real man, and she loved how he treated her as an equal, as if she was actually an interesting person. That was new for Tasmin.

He seemed too good to be true - devilishly attractive, amusing, caring and successful - and when he had placed his hands on her stomach that night before, she had felt an electric jolt of desire zap through her. She blushed at the memory. What was wrong with her? At a family dinner, way too pregnant, getting turned on by a guy as he felt her child. She groaned aloud in the empty apartment.

Hormonal desire apart - because she refused to concede it could be anything more than a crazy flush of oestrogen - she could not trust her judgement.

Once, Logan had made her skin tingle and body burn with need too, and she had been blind to every red flag because of it. That lapse in judgement had almost cost her her life, and now she had the hormonal hots over his brother. They say blood is thicker than water, and if that is true, craving Lachlan is like jumping from the frying pan to the fire.

She just had to get through the next few weeks, until the baby was born, and her equilibrium returned.

CHAPTER 15 - LACHLAN

It took a sustained, conscious effort, but Lachlan managed to keep his growing feelings for Tasmin hidden. His affection for this quiet, beautiful stranger mystified him, but he was careful to act as normally as possible, which was difficult when the mere mention of her name brought a flush of heat to his body.

He visited Dawn and Lewis several times over the month, and as the media eagerly grabbed hold of the Government's announcement of a partnership with the newly launched Lewis Wolfe Foundation the family was suddenly thrust into the limelight.

It seemed pandemic weary reporters across the country were desperate for positive news, so Lewis and Lachlan embarked on a hectic week of interviews and guest appearance, all from the safety of Lewis' luxurious home office. It seemed to Lachlan that a TV studio had appeared overnight, and while he sometimes lagged at the pace, his father seemed more energised and elated each day. They were fortunate to have Tim to guide them through the maze of interview requests, despite the Party having their traditional favourite news outlets; Lachlan was sure he was not endearing himself to Jonathon Carter or his media mogul mates, but it felt good to call the shots. His proposal had caused such an upturn in the Government's approval rating that, right now, Lachlan was beyond reproach. He was not naive enough to expect it to continue, and knew he was burning some powerful bridges, but he was determined to sort that out later. For now, the Foundation and the vaccine hubs were his top priority, during work hours at least. He and Tasmin crossed paths regularly at the mansion, and once at a celebratory lunch hosted by his parents, but he kept a respectful distance. In reality at least; in his dreams she came to him most nights, and he woke with a delicious longing, that the harsh reality of day slapped out of him with disappointing regularity. Tasmin bloomed before his eyes. As her due date approached her face and limbs softened in anticipation of the birth, and although he thought she often looked sleepy, she was radiantly beautiful. He saw her early one morning without make-up, and she stunned him. He saw her emerge from the Wolfe's swimming pool, dripping and rotund with child, and thought she was the most exquisite woman he had ever seen. It made no sense to him at all, but he was powerless to ignore her.

He tried not to hover over her when they were together, but the thought of her facing the birth alone had started to worry him. Surely, something so momentous was meant to be shared? Isn't that what all those parenting classes on TV said? That everyone needed a birthing partner? There was no way he could offer, but he worried over it all the same.

Lachlan was bent over Lewis's desk late in the evening, as they went through the list of final interviews scheduled for the following day. Tim had advised them to give a first round of interviews, then withdraw and release good news stories once they started to get some evidence and testimonials flowing in from the project. Lachlan was relieved; the pace had been exhausting and he needed to return to the House and catch up on the demands of his constituents. Lewis, on the other hand, had ceded day-to-day control of his empire to his managing director, and being the Foundation's operations manager was to become his main role. Lachlan felt it was an ideal situation, and thought himself fortunate again, that Lewis had leapt at his idea.

When Dawn stepped into the office from the pool side doorway, they both looked up. Lachlan loved the way Lewis' eyes lit up when they alighted on his wife. Once, as a jaded playboy that look had made Lachlan smirk with disdain, but now, if made him feel safe, confident in the love his parents shared.

"It's time," she said simply, and for a moment Lachlan was confused.

"Time?" he asked.

Lewis on the other hand simply rose and pressed a button on the intercom to signal their driver.

He turned to Lachlan. "Son, when your mother says, 'It's time' it means there is a baby on the way." He looked to Dawn, smiling in the doorway.

"There is a baby on the way," she confirmed. "Tasmin is at the hospital and Fairy is with her. We can go as well, although there will be limits as to how many people are allowed inside."

During the height of the pandemic there had been countless sorrow-filled stories of people giving birth alone, enduring surgeries alone, and dying in isolation, as hospitals scrambled to keep virus VS-202 at bay. Lachlan suddenly felt uncomfortable, and out of place. His instincts told him to rush to the hospital and never leave Tasmin's side, but in reality, he would not be permitted into the labour ward. In reality, he was nothing to her. Fairy and Dawn were her family - he was just an outsider.

"You head off Dad," he said, eager to get them on their way to her. "We are finished up here anyway, and you can update me from the hospital." Please keep me updated; every minute. That remained unsaid.

"Are you sure you don't want to join us?" Dawn's voice was soft and kind, but Lachlan was not sure why she offered.

"Me? Of course not. No. You two go and we'll be in touch." To avoid any further questions, he headed down the carpeted hall and outside to his waiting car. In his own apartment he poured a scotch over ice and connected his phone to the charging cord. He checked the volume settings in case it rang, and he missed it, then he switched on the TV for background noise. The late-night news channel was running a replay of an interview he and Lewis had given earlier that day, and it was too disconcerting to watch himself on the screen, so Lachlan flicked it to a banal sit-com.

He had a shower and brewed a pot of coffee. He replied to some emails and tried to read through some House correspondence, but his concentration wandered. He fried some bacon and toasted thick slices of Turkish bread, but the assembled BLT sandwich tasted bland. He sipped a second scotch then tipped it down the sink, in case he needed to drive, and poured a strong coffee instead. He paced the penthouse, pausing to look over the city lights, remembering how dark the streets below had seemed during the worst months of lockdown. At least now some taillights once again shone in the darkness, but city living had certainly lost a lot of appeal for many, himself included, he realised with a start.

His apartment had been chosen because of its location - right in the heart of the city and close to the action. He had access to all kinds of deliveries with just a phone call, and every club and bar worth visiting was within his reach. The best parties and galas were held around here and that had been the motivation when he purchased the sleek unit.

He looked around now and took in the glass and polished stone decor with new eyes. It looked as stylish and expensive as ever, but tonight it also seemed cold, and Lachlan knew with sudden clarity

that he would be looking for somewhere new very
soon. His city living days were done; he was a different
man now. Maybe he could find a gem like Sara's.
The thought of his sister made him move across to the
table and open the email program on his laptop.
His message was simple.
"Dear Sara,
I miss your face.
Love Lach"
He attached a photo of them both at her farm,
wearing gumboots and covered in filthy mud and sent
it off. He was sipping from his coffee cup when a
reply pinged back.
"Any news on the baby?
Miss you too.
I told you I hate that photo. Get rid of it.
Love S"
The email made him smile. Sara would never admit
her shortcomings, but he was glad to hear from her.
He sent his mother an email, knowing it would ping
on her phone - Sara had given him the perfect excuse
to ask the question he had agonised over for hours.
"Sara and I are wondering how it's all going," he
wrote, the white lie flying from his fingertips. "Any
news?" He added Sara's email address to the message
so Dawn could update them both easily and sent it off
into the mysterious place emails sailed to. He wished
he could materialise at Tasmin's side as quickly as the
'whoosh' noise the email made. He muted the laptop

instead; in the dim room the screen lighting up would announce a new message anyway.

He was into a second cup of coffee before his mother replied.

"I have been in with Tamsin, and everything is going as planned. She is progressing well, so we have decided to stay here with her. Baby's heart rate is wonderful, and the midwife says probably another couple of hours.

X"

Lachlan gulped. Hours? Jesus Christ, he had never considered the length of labour. When Sara had the girls, he had been in New York for one and holidaying in Queensland for the other, so the time between "We're going to the hospital" and "She's born" had not ever really registered. The thought of Tasmin panting and groaning like the sweaty women in those grainy Year 10 science class movies made him feel nauseous. God, he wished he could help her.

He fell into a fitful sleep, awkwardly folded into one of his reclining armchairs but when his phone chirped the arrival of a new email his eyes sprung open. Groggily he opened the phone and his screen filled with a picture of a smiling Tasmin holding a small red-faced bundle in a pink blanket.

"She's here," his mother's message read. "4.22am. 3268 grams. Simply beautiful. She looks like Sara as a baby." Lachlan was not sure how that final piece of information would go down, but if anything could bring his sister round, it would be this tiny scrap of a human.

Lachlan gazed at the photo for a long time, taking in every inch of Tasmin's face, from the twin ruddy cheeks to the wide smile. She looked happy, serene, and even more beautiful than ever. She looked exhausted and elated all at once.

He padded to his room and lay down on the bed to sleep, taking the phone with him.

When Lachlan woke the next morning, he felt energised despite the late night, and after firing off some instructions to staff to reschedule their last interviews he made his way to the hospital. At the entrance of the hospital, he went through the VS-202 checkpoint; his testing paperwork was checked, as was his temperature, and he sanitised his hands before donning a facemask. The nurse on duty at the checkpoint recognised him and almost instantly tears filled her eyes, visible above her mask.

"Thank you," she said simply. "Thank you for getting the vaccine roll out happening. You have no idea what it's been like but thank you."

Lachlan was halted in his tracks, cemented to the spot by the weight of her words. He was unable to find any words, so he simply nodded but as he passed by her, he reached out and placed a hand on her arm. She placed her own, latex glove encased hand over his and through the protective layers they shared an unspoken moment.

He again showed his test paperwork at the reception
desk as he gathered directions to the maternity wing
and used his phone's camera to scan into the hospital's
tracing application. It was second nature now. He
stopped at the gift shop to buy a garish helium
balloon, printed with rainbows and in the shape of a
unicorn, and a scented candle for Tasmin, and made
his way upstairs. The horned horse bobbed
ridiculously behind him.

Lewis was seated in the waiting room, and Lachlan
thought he looked tired, but knew if he queried his
father would never admit it. Once he had checked
Tasmin was ok for himself he would take both his
parents home to rest.

He shook hands with his father, who gestured towards
a closed door.

"Go in," he said. "They are waiting for you. It's only
your mother in there right now. Fairy will be back
later, once she has had some sleep."

He felt self-conscious as he entered the small private
room, and hovered in the doorway for a moment,
regretting the balloon purchase. It clashed with the
large bunch of white roses and fern leaves in a vase
beside the bed. Lewis had much better taste than he,
Lachlan admitted to himself as he closed the door
behind him.

Tasmin was sitting in the bed before him, freshly
showered and smelling of flowers. Her hair was piled
atop her head but some wisps around her face had
escaped, and they trailed down the side of her

alabaster cheeks. Dawn was seated in a wide soft-looking armchair placed in the corner of the room, hugging a small mewling bundle to her chest. She had her face close to the babies and was murmuring softly to her. She did not stop, gently rocking the infant and whispering in her ear, but her eyes met Lachlan's and she smiled.

"Oh Lachy. She is perfect."

Lachlan laughed softly. "Of course she is Dawn. You wouldn't have it any other way." He and Tasmin shared a smile and when she gestured to a hard backed seat beside her, he took it. He handed the balloon to her awkwardly.

"This one is dumb," he admitted, before handing her the candle. "Hopefully, this is a bit more… ah, appropriate."

Tasmin giggled. "Oh, I don't know," she said.

"Perhaps Rose will love unicorns."

Dawn's head shot up. "Rose is that her name? That's lovely." She peered down at the child with obvious adoration, and Lachlan realised he was among the first to know the baby's name. He flushed with inexplicable pride.

"Rose Dawn," Tasmin announced. "Her name is Rose Dawn Wolfe, if that's ok with you Dawn." Lachlan glanced at his mother and could almost feel the emotion coming off her in waves.

"Dawn?" she said. "After me?"

Tasmin nodded. "Rose is my middle name and it's also Fairy's real name, so it works in perfectly." She glanced at Lachlan. "I will talk to Lewis about using Wolfe as her surname, in case there are any, well, objections." Lachlan knew she was referring to Sara. "But," Tasmin continued, "the midwife has taken a cheek swab of both Rose and Dawn, and we will have paternity results confirmed next week." She spoke in an unusual business-like fashion, and Lachlan felt sad that she had to endure this part of his family. He knew their solicitor - and no doubt Sara - had insisted.

"Well," he said, trying to sound cheerful. "That's all that taken care of, so the rest of us can just enjoy Dawn and Fairy fighting over poor little Rosie." He grinned at his mother who sniffed haughtily.

"Rosie," Tasmin repeated softly, looking at him with tired eyes. "Rosie sounds beautiful."

Lachlan did not stay long. He carefully held the baby and marvelled at her perfect features, a mix of Sara's high forehead and Tasmin's blush lips. His visit confirmed both mother and child were well, and when he could see Tasmin was getting tired, he decided to leave. Dawn agreed to stay only until Fairy returned and then she and Lewis would head home soon to rest. With everything in order Lachlan stood and placed the baby in Tasmin's waiting arms. She looked so natural, sitting there against the pillows with her child nestled against her heart. Lachlan's own heart swelled with emotion. He dared to lean forward and place a soft kiss on Tasmin's temple.

"Call me if you need anything," he said quietly. "And if it's ok, I'd love to come back tomorrow."

Tasmin looked at him with her clear blue eyes the colour of the morning sky.

"I'd like that," she said.

When Lachlan returned the following day, the room was full. Fairy sat in the cosy armchair holding the baby as she squawked tightly, Dawn was seated beside Tasmin on the narrow bed, while Lewis hovered at the window. Tasmin was crying. The scene was in stark contrast to the gentle vibe that had misted through the room yesterday.

"What's going on?" Lachlan was startled. "What's wrong? Is Rosie ok?"

"Baby Rose is just fine," Fairy answered. "But Mumma is a bit emotional, that's all. Hormones and stuff, you know."

Lachlan experienced a rush of emotion that swept through him with uncomfortable unfamiliarity. He wanted to rush to the weeping beauty before him, pushing everyone else aside, to hold her in his arms and keep her safe. He wanted to sooth the frizzing hair at her brow and kiss her until the tears evaporated. He wanted to snatch Rosie and gather them both to his chest. He felt a rage inside him that Tasmin felt anything other than joy, and the anger swirled and curdled with a confusion that kept him rooted to the one spot.

Fairy looked at him from the soft armchair, her head cocked to one side, as Tasmin sniffled quietly beside her.

"You right mate?" she asked. "You look a bit out of sorts. Don't worry about any of this," Fairy gestured around the room, taking in the tears of both mother and daughter. "This happens. Tasmin's milk is coming in, so she's feeling pretty uncomfortable and this little one is upset because Mumma's upset." Fairy looked down at Rosie who was still waving tiny furious fists in the air but had stopped protesting so much. Watching the child with love, Fairy continued.

"Bub hasn't had a decent feed all day either. It's the engorgement, you know?"

The old woman looked squarely at Lachlan and to his horror he felt the colour slide from his face.

Engorgement? What the actual fuck was he doing here?

Unable to stop his eyes from darting madly about the bizarre scene before him, he babbled an excuse about coming back at a better time and escaped backwards into the hallway. He took great care to keep his eyes from meeting Tasmin's or from falling downwards to her chest, and he was certain he heard a low chuckle come from Fairy's side of the room as he fled.

In the corridor he leaned shakily against the wall, grateful for the wide timber handrail that steadied him. Taking a deep breath he straightened and strode to the elevator, determined to pull himself together and ignore the depth of feeling that had so recently taken hold of him. He stepped into the lift as another man called out. "Hold it! Hold the lift please!"

Reflexively Lachlan thrust an arm into the space between the closing doors, which yielded and allowed his fellow passenger to rush in.

"Cheers," the man said. "Thought I wasn't going to make it for a sec."

Lachlan offered him a wobbly half smile; he still felt awkward and uneasy, and the stranger seemed to sense it immediately.

"Your first?" he asked kindly. Lachlan was puzzled, and it showed, so the man continued. "Your first baby? I don't mean to be rude, but you have that kind of shell-shocked look we all get when it hits us." He chuckled.

"Shell shock?" Even to his own ears Lachlan sounded dense, like he was half drunk or battling a monster hangover.

"Yeah - shell shocked. You know, the moment when we realise that we are a father now, we have all this responsibility, and suddenly we aren't all that important anymore." The man shrugged easily, and Lachlan guessed they would be a similar age. "Don't get me wrong," he carried on, "It is absolutely the very best thing that will ever happen to you. We have three kids now and I love the little guys but it's just a lot, when you actually realise, you know?" His question was rhetorical, but Lachan was nevertheless relieved when the lift juddered to a halt on the ground floor, and the doors slid open noiselessly. He hung back and let the man emerge before him - he did not even want to consider trying to explain his situation right now.

"Oh, I'm not the dad," he would have to say. "I'm the brother of the long-lost bastard son my mum left behind and I think I'm in love with his widow, who is upstairs crying in agony because her breasts are engorged, apparently." Christ what a mess.
His silence did not perturb the stranger who strode into the carpark, blithely climbing into a wide four-wheel-drive, with a row of car seats lining the back seat.
Lachlan sat in his own car for a long time, trying to unpack his feelings. Did he love Tasmin? Could he really be in love with her, or was it all wild, mad emotions tied up with Rosie's birth and the new closeness he was sharing with his father?
Shaking his head to empty it, Lachlan started the engine and slid the sleek sedan into traffic with a roar of the powerful engine. His club would help him forget all this.
Hours later Lachlan found himself full of expensive whiskey, and cheap pick-up lines, both of which kept the party goers around him mesmerised. He chose a tall dark-skinned beauty with slender hips and a mess of wild black curls. She could not be further from Tasmin if he tried. And he had tried - very hard - avoiding any titian haired women, in his quest to exorcise his dead brother's widow from his overworked brain. She persisted, invading his thoughts, and distracting him as brazen men and women sized him up and flirted outrageously; Lachlan

found himself comparing them all to her alabaster, natural beauty.

Until the Amazonian woman strode across the crowded club floor and stood before him.

"Dance with me." It was not a question. Lachlan stood and followed her to a dark corner of the small dance floor, allowing himself to touch the small of her back as she swayed in front of him.

She wore a cream-coloured silk sheath with thin straps that swam about her, emphasising her slender form. The silk moved across her small breasts, enticing her nipples to stand proud against the delicate fabric, as she pulled Lachlan to her.

She mimicked the smooth jazz music that surrounded them, swaying her hips, and moving her body against him, the silk fabric sliding sensuously between them. They moved against each other, hands sliding up and down as they explored arms, chests, buttocks, oblivious to the crowds dancing around them. The music swelled and fell, and with it Lachan's desire rose; the whiskey and this woman had stripped away all inhibitions.

So entranced was he that Lachlan almost did not notice the other woman until she slid one hand beneath his jacket to encircle his body. As she swayed into view, she leant across and kissed his dance partner on the side of her dewy throat. Lachlan felt the desire rise in him as the two women gestured for him to follow them.

In the suite Lachlan fell back onto the bed as one
woman then the next crawled over him, sweeping his
clothes from him and shimmering from their own.
The trio gasped and grasped at each other, tongues
colliding and nails biting into flesh.
Closing his eyes Lachlan relaxed into a soft moan as
lips moved across his taut stomach and down, down,
down until…
Tasmin leapt into his mind.
Lachlan's eyes flew open and in disgust he scrambled
to move away from the writhing naked bodies of the
two women. Suddenly sober, he backed away, escaped
the bed, and fled to the luxurious bathroom. He
doubted the women missed him at all.
Standing under the steaming shower he allowed the
hot needles to sting his flesh as the small room filled
with steam. Lachlan felt guilty and ashamed, and more
confused than ever.

CHAPTER 16 - TASMIN

It had been an incredible few months since Rosie's birth. Cocooned in the sunny apartment mother and daughter had slowly learned to trust each other and Tasmin swore her heart would burst with the sheer volume of the love she felt for her child. Ignoring Fairy and Dawn, Tasmin dragged the beautiful, handcrafted cradle, gifted by Lewis, from the small nursery across the hall into her own room. She placed it beside her own bed and together, the two would lie and gaze at each other; Rosie content and full of milk, and Tasmin with abject wonder.

Her life was charmed, this she knew and appreciated, and she could not thank Lewis and Dawn enough for giving her the opportunity to ease into caring for her baby slowly and calmly. It was all so new, but cocoon of the Wolfe's wealth gave her time to adjust, and simply revel in the wonder of her child. Her meals arrived like clockwork, courtesy of a delicious food delivery service and her living costs were being covered. She had attempted to discuss the arrangement with Lewis on one of his visits, but he had brushed her concerns away.

"There will be time to get on your feet later, my dear," he had said carefully. "For now, it is my honour to give you this time to share with your daughter." He had winked at her then, and flashed her a rare, cheeky grin. "And it makes me quite the hero in my wife's eyes, which is always beneficial!"

Tasmin strolled in the sunshine with Rosie tucked up tightly in their fancy new pram, and window shopped around the neighbourhood. She enjoyed coffee at outdoor cafes and allowed older couples to coo over her beautiful baby with pride. She video called her delighted parents and sister and tearfully introduced Rosie to them, and even travelled out to Fairy's for a visit each week or so, carefully averting her gaze from the empty house next door.

Fairy understood the only risk to this bright bubble of happiness was the guilt which gnawed relentlessly at her soul and tried to convince her to move on.

"Can't be helped now," she announced the last time they spoke on the telephone. "What's done is done, and it was a case of you or him, I bet my left nut on that." Tasmin had needed to stifle an ill-timed giggle at that one, but Fairy had continued unperturbed.

"Besides, if you want to admit anything to anyone, you'd be dropping me in the turds as well, and I'm too old to be sent to gaol."

Tasmin knew she was right. She knew Logan had been one bad trip away from seriously hurting her - or worse - and they thought of the harm he could have caused Rosie filled her with terror. He was a dangerous and damaged man, and during the pandemic it had seemed normal life had changed forever. Back then, she had only had herself to rely on, once everyone else abandoned those in need, to simply survive. But now, life was slowly beginning to return to normal, and like a breath of fresh air Lachan drifted effortlessly into her days.

Sometimes he called by, unannounced, but with an uncanny sense of timings. He would step into the small apartment and swoop Rosie into his arms and send Tasmin to the bathroom to enjoy a steaming hot shower in peace. He would arrive at her door armed with a large fresh juice or a new magazine to read distractedly while feeding Rosie. He helped her wade through the kindergarten brochures Dawn smothered her with, laughing about his mother's obsessive nature all the while. He bought Sara and her daughters to meet Rosie and broke the awkwardness with his constant chatter; the DNA results had proven what Tasmin had always known, and the official looking letter had melted Sara's attitude towards them. A little, anyway.

Bethany and Ava squabbled over who would hold Rosie first and Tasmin watched Lachlan calm them both and gently oversee the passage of her precious daughter from one set of eagerly waiting arms to the next.

"Thank you," she had said quietly to Sara, and noted that the older woman almost jumped at the words. She looked at Tasmin with puzzlement.

"For what?" she asked.

"For coming here." Tasmin's words were soft. She did not want Lachlan or the girls to hear them, lest this conversation go badly. "For visiting and for allowing your girls to know Rosie. Right now, they are the only family my baby has, and I am grateful you are here." At this she looked up at Sara, meeting her gaze with a bravery she did not know she had. "Thank you," Tasmin repeated.

Sara had not replied, other than with a tight smile, not quite friendly, but a definite improvement. Tasmin had decided to take that as a win.

Rosie was crying relentlessly and Tasmin paced backwards and forwards across the plush carpet, jiggling the baby up and down, up and down, crooning nonsense and trying to ignore the ache deep in her back. After a few nights of broken sleep, the crying had now been going on for hours and Tasmin felt exhausted. Her eyes were gritty with lack of sleep and her stomach growled with hunger. So far, since giving in at 5am and reluctantly dragging them both out of bed, Tasmin had bathed Rosie, walked her around the block in the chilly morning air, fed her, held her, put her down, picked her back up again, lay with her, sloshed her in a warm bath and tried feeding her some more, but still Rosie howled. Her tiny face was red with anger and effort and Tasmin felt like she looked the same. The child was inconsolable and Tasmin was at a loss. The hours felt like days, and she was starting to think something must be very, very wrong. *Surely this wasn't normal? To just cry like this for so long? Maybe Rosie was ill? Oh, God! Maybe she was ill!*

The doorbell cut through Tasmin's panicked thoughts, and she carried the still sobbing child on her hip to the door.

Lachlan stood in the hallway, and at the sight of both mother and child he smiled warmly at them.

"Tough day?" he asked, stepping past Tasmin and into the apartment. It was so natural to have him here now that Tasmin barely registered, and simply pushed the door shut behind him. She was still jiggling Rosie up and down but was becoming more panicked by the moment.

"I think she's sick," she blurted out, loudly and abruptly. "She won't stop crying and I think something must be wrong." To her ears Tasmin knew she sounded whiney and frantic, but she did not care. Not one bit; she was too busy trying not to cry herself. Lachlan immediately put down the two coffees he was carrying on the stone kitchen island and held his arms out for the baby. Tasmin hesitated - what kind of mother just hands their child over when it gets hard? Lachlan sensed her trepidation and smiled, stepping closer to her, and carefully taking the baby from her. He cocooned Rosie to his chest and as he did, Tasmin was hit with the intoxicating scent of him. It was not just cologne, it was his musky aftershave, the soapy freshness of his hair and the heady caffeine aroma that combined to deliver her a knockout blow. Her insides melted and she was temporarily taken aback.

Rosie soon brought her crashing back to reality, letting out a wail and arching her back angrily against Lachlan's embrace.

"You see?" Tasmin cried. "She is never this upset. Never. I've tried everything." Like a maniac she rattled off the list of the mornings attempts to calm her child, as Lachlan calmly lowered himself into the armchair beside her. He lay the protesting Rosie on her back along his strong thighs, and as she screamed, he peered into her mouth.

"Teething," he announced.

Tasmin stared at him. "What?"

"I think she's teething," he repeated and Tasmin marvelled at his composure. Both she and Rosie had done nothing but yell at him since he arrived, yet here he was, quietly sitting down to diagnose the problem. He gently probed the baby's tiny mouth and as she clamped down on his finger he nodded, then winked at Tasmin.

"Her gums are really red and swollen and I think I can just about feel one breaking though, the poor poppet." He reached over and grasped Tasmin's hand with his own and drew her near, so she too could feel the culprit of today's unrest; a tiny shard of tooth. Tasmin felt like a fool.

"But... but she is only five months old," Tasmin exclaimed, yet even as the words fell from her lips, she knew Lachlan was right. She had hungrily read every parenting manual available, and yet in her exhaustion the thought had not even occurred to her.

Unbidden, hot tears sprang to her eyes and the image of Lachlan, and her child wavered before her as if she were under water.

"Don't cry!" Lachlan sounded almost as panicked as she had felt earlier. "Please Tas. Don't cry. There is nothing to cry about. Honestly, it's all ok."

He was right. Of course, he was right, but the tears escaped regardless and slid down her cheek until she angrily wiped at them. *What was wrong with her?*

"It's just…" she began, then faltered. It sounded so stupid. Lachlan would think she was stupid.

"What?" He seemed genuinely interested, and he reached out to hold her hand, which now sat enveloped by his long, strong fingers.

A hiccupping sob escaped her. "She's growing up too fast!" The tears fell freely now, and despite feeling ridiculous, Tasmin was powerless to stem the flood of emotion coursing through her body.

Lachlan leaned near, the baby at his chest and wrapped his arm around Tasmin.

"Shhhhhhh," he crooned into her hair as she gave in and relaxed against him, drenching his lapel with emotion-filled tears. Mother and daughter wept as Lachlan patiently held them both, until the tears subsided.

First to settle was little Rosie, who quietened and stared curiously at Tasmin, her sweet face looking from Lachlan's to hers with interest. When Tasmin realised she was the only one in the room still crying she pulled away with embarrassment.

"Oh God, I'm so sorry," she said, wiping her eyes on the back of her hands and trying in vain to stem the watery flow from both her eyes and nose. She must look and absolute sight, she realised with horror. "I… um … I'll be right back." Leaving Rosie in her wake she fled to the bathroom.

The mirror confirmed every suspicion; her face and throat were blotchy from crying and her nose dribbled unattractively. Her fringe was matted to her sweaty brow, where she had crushed against Lachlan yet at the crown of her head the golden locks were a dishevelled bird's nest. The overall effect was horrific and Tasmin started at herself in disbelief.

Right now, in her very living room, stood one of the most attractive, powerful eligible men she had ever laid eyes on, and here she was, a mess of a human, prone to dramatic bouts of despair and tears like a mid-century fair maiden.

She scrubbed at her face then brushed her teeth hurriedly, scrambling through the drawers of the vanity with one hand, searching for a brush to tame her hair. She found a comb and as she began to drag the knots from her hair, she caught sight of herself in the mirror.

Tasmin stopped. What was she doing? What on Earth was she doing?

The comb clattered to the basin as Tasmin trembled. She started at her reflection. Was she seriously trying to pretty herself up for Lachlan? The girl in the mirror looked back at her scornfully. Surely, she did not forget who she was, what she had done? A fancy new home and kind new family might be a beautiful illusion, but the reflection was there to remind Tasmin that she was - at her core - a piece of murdering trash. Nothing more.

She returned to the living room, and saw Rosie was peacefully sleeping in her rocker by the large windows that overlooked the park. Despite herself Tasmin smiled, relieved the crying had stopped.

"Thank you," she said quietly. She moved to the kitchen, placing the wide stone countertop between them. Lachlan did not reply but pushed the tall coffee cup towards her.

"I gave this a quick zap in the microwave to reheat it," he said, "but it's still pretty good." He raised his own cup to her then took a sip, as if to encourage her to do the same. She did, and - once again - he was right. The coffee was silky and hot, and she felt it slither some energy into her tired soul.

"I'm just going to pop down to the chemist and grab you, well, Rosie, some teething gel and painkillers," Lachlan said, inching towards the door. Tasmin thought he looked like he wanted to escape, so she nodded.

Tasmin was dreaming of a beach with waves lapping at the shore, and children laughing in the background. She thought she was at some sort of party because she could hear cheering in the distance and the delicious aroma of roasting meat was wafting across the beach to her. Her stomach rumbling in anticipation and her eyes flew open.

Across the room Lachlan grinned at her. "Hungry, huh?"

She struggled to sit up, disorientated, and groggy, slowly realising she was in the apartment, Had she fallen asleep on the lounge? Rosie was sitting contentedly on Lachlan's lap and the television on the wall quietly played a football match, and each time the crowd cheered, she giggled delightedly.

Lachlan shrugged' "I think she's a sport's fan," he said. Tasmin looked at them both, then around the room and realised it was now dark outside. Lachlan had left the drapes open, and the city glittered below them. He followed her gaze.

"Sorry I didn't close them," he said. "The view during sunset was too good to miss."

Tasmin nodded as if she agreed, although she usually closed them as soon as the days began to end; the open curtains made her feel exposed and unsafe, even this high up.

She started to speak, to apologise for flaking out but her stomach rumbled again, and Lachlan sprang up. In a few long strides he had crossed the room and plopped Rosie in her lap. Tasmin immediately drew the baby towards her and breathed in her smell. How she loved this child.

"Dinner arrived while you were napping," Lachlan said. "It's roast beef so I have had it warming in the oven for you." From the kitchen Tasmin could hear him rattling crockery and diving though the cutlery drawer. For such a graceful man, he sure made a racket.

He bought her a steaming plate of mouth-watering food, and once he realised she did not want to give up Rosie, he cut the meal into bite sized pieces so she could eat one-handed.

After a few mouthfuls Tasmin began to awaken properly, and looked across to Lachlan once more, where he sat, engrossed in the game. He looked like he belonged.

She cleared her throat. "I am sorry Lachlan," she began, "for being such a basket case. I do appreciate everything you do for me." Lachlan turned to face her, but Tasmin kept her eyes averted. "I appreciate everything your family has done for me, and I will make it all up to you one day." She had vowed this often to herself but had not ever voiced it aloud. "I am going to make a proper life for Rosie, and I will make sure your parents can always be proud of her." A crowd cheered softly in the background, and Tasmin appreciated the sentiment.

Lachlan was quiet for a moment.

"What are you doing? He asked eventually.

Tasmin was confused. "Pardon?"

"You're talking to me - at me - like I'm a bloody stranger. What do you mean 'we'll be proud of Rosie'? Of course we will!" Lachlan sounded almost angry. Tasmin swallowed and adjusted Rosie, who was reaching for one of the tender morsels of roasted pumpkin. It hurt to think her words made him upset, but she could not allow herself to be distracted by him.

Lachlan took a deep breath and exhaled noisily. It seemed to Tasmin that he was working up to something, and when he crossed the room and sat on the carpet at her feet she was instantly on guard. What was he doing?

"Tasmin," he began. "I care for you." The words entered her heart, where they burst and shot heat through her veins. Lachlan avoided her gaze, watching Rosie instead, but his words were definitely meant for Tasmin, and she was terrified.

"I don't have a good track record with women. I don't have a good track record with relationships of any kind, if I am really honest." Tasmin could see he was nervous; his legs were crossed under him like a schoolboy, and they jiggled anxiously. From her vantage point on the sofa Tasmin felt his vulnerability in the quiet, deliberate way he spoke.

"The virus, the lockdowns, you, Rosie, the Foundation, even finding out about Logan … all those things have changed me. I am a different person. I know that sounds cliched, but I am not the same person I was before the pandemic." He looked at her

now, his dark eyes shining in the reflected glow from
the television. Without his words to fill the shortening
space between them, the room was so quiet Tasmin
was certain he could hear her shuddering heartbeats.
"I don't know what it means, and I don't know how it
could work, and I don't even know how it happened,
but I think I am in love with you Tasmin." Blood
rushed to her ears and her cheeks flushed from the
effort of not falling into his arms.
"No scrap that," he said and instantly disappointment
hit Tasmin like a punch to the gut, until he finished his
sentence. "I *know* I love you."
Tasmin felt her heart grow heavy as a tight knot
formed in the pit of her stomach. She looked down to
where Lachlan sat, taking in the sincerity in his eyes.
She knew he was telling the truth. If she was honest,
she had known it for months because she had seen the
love grow before her, but she also knew what she
must do.
"No Lachlan," she said.

CHAPTER 17 - LACHLAN

Sweat dripped from Lachlan's soaked fringe onto the digital display of the high-tech treadmill, as he pushed his body harder and harder. His lungs ached with the effort and the soles of his feet protested with every step; he had been slogging on this bastard machine for almost an hour now, music heavy with bass thundering in his ears, loud enough to block out every thought.

Almost loud enough.

But not quite.

He missed Tasmin every day, every moment. Weeks had passed since the day in her apartment when his new world came crashing down around him, and yet it seemed like only yesterday. The stabbing in his chest whenever his mind strayed to replay those words did not lessen.

"No Lachlan," she had said. "No. It is not possible. You can't love me."

He had protested, of course he had. He had tried to explain how his love had grown slowly until it could no longer be ignored, but how certain he was of that love. It was - is, he corrected sadly - nothing like he had ever experienced before.

His pleas had fallen limply between them, she on the sofa holding Rosie to her like a shield and he, sitting - begging - on the floor at her feet. He was even too heartbroken to feel any sort of embarrassment at his behaviour. He cared for little except her response.

Her rejection of him was peppered with examples of her life with Logan, and Lachlan listened in horrified silence as she recalled the cruelty and fear in a dull monotone. Rage rose in him - if Logan were still alive, he could have killed him with his own hands - and then fell, replaced with a deep regret at all Tasmin had endured. *Thank Christ for Fairy*, Lachlan thought, finally understanding the bond between the two unlikely friends.

When Tasmin was finally spent, she had looked at him with such sadness that Lachlan was sure he could hear his heart break.

"No Lachlan. I have Rosie to think about now. She is all that matters, and I will not risk any of my bad decisions affecting her." Her words were curt, formal, and business-like, and so unlike her that Lachlan knew she had made her decision.

He stood, told her that his feelings would not change, kissed Rosie softly on her head and left.

He had seen them rarely since. He avoided visiting the Wolfe mansion if he thought they may be around and escaped to Sara and Tim's place as often as he could.

He and Tim took vigorous hikes across the hills that bordered their land, and spoke at length about Tasmin, the family, his lost brother, and the whole blasted mess, but little changed for Lachlan. He still loved Tasmin, and she still did not love him back. He threw himself into his work in the Senate and with the Foundation, shadowing his father across the country when he was able. The speed in which the vaccine rollout was progressing was incredible, and it was the only shining light in Lachlan's otherwise dim life. He was immensely proud of the work he and Lewis were undertaking and relished the closeness they had developed.

Outside his work at the House and at the Foundation Lachlan worked out in the gym. He signed onto a gruelling training regime with an ex-Army sergeant, who barked orders at him and pushed him further than he thought possible. The daily effort seared an ache in his muscles that rivalled the one in his heart, and helped him fall into an exhausted, dreamless sleep each night. He had not been near his club or his old drinking acquaintances since leaving Tasmin's apartment.

His phone pinged as a message arrived, and he paused the treadmill to slow its speed to allow him to check it. It was from Dawn.

"Dinner tonight 7pm. I've checked your schedule with Harry, so I know you are available. See you then. X."

Lachlan cursed his assistant's honesty under his breath as he killed power to the treadmill and headed for the sauna. He still had demons to exorcise before he could face Dawn.

When he strode into the kitchen of his parent's vast home that evening the sight of Tasmin sitting at the informal eating area with Bethany, the eldest of his nieces, caused him to falter momentarily. She looked incredible, her hair piled messily atop her head, which was bent towards the colouring book she and Bethany were painstakingly decorating. Rosie sat beside them, firmly strapped into a highchair, happily destroying a portion of soft banana between her chubby fingers. Bethany spotted him first. "Uncle Lachy!" she squealed, springing from her chair to leap into his arms. Ava came next, summoned by her sister's loud cries, and Lachlan was grateful for the distraction both the children provided. Sara and Dawn followed Ava into the large kitchen, plopping down trays of barbecued meats onto the timber tabletop.

Lachlan raised an eyebrow. "Barbecue?" he asked. Barbecue was far from the Wolfe family regular cuisine.

Sara swatted at him playfully. "Not fancy enough for you Senator?" she mocked, before leaning up to kiss him on the cheek. She faced him squarely. "Nice to see you Lach," she said, squeezing his arm gently. "We've missed you." Lachlan had the good grace to feel gently scolded for his absence. None of this was their fault.

Lewis and Tim joined them, creating another diversion and the loud greetings and back slapping meant he could avoid speaking with Tasmin for just a little longer. He dreaded the thought of being ignored by her.

In the weeks since his declaration he had seen Tasmin twice, both from afar, both at family gatherings to support the Foundations, so avoiding her had been painful, but easily achieved. This - an intimate family lunch, a barbecue, for heaven's sake - was going to be a lot harder.

Dawn carried bowl after bowl from the large refrigerator, covering the table with bowls of salads, pasta, and crusty bread rolls. Lachlan enquired after Marg and learned she was on a well-earned week away to visit her family. A lessening of travel restrictions in some states had finally made long awaited reunions among loved ones possible.

"So this is all your doing Dawn?" he asked, raising a good-natured eyebrow at his mother, and indicating the casual feast spread in front of them.

Dawn raised an elegant brow in return. "Shut up and eat Lachlan," she answered tartly. "I have made the salads, Sara brought the rolls with her from that little Italian bakery we like, and Tim and your father cooked all the meat on Lewis' new barbecue." She beamed proudly at her husband, but Lachlan was amazed.

"You have a barbecue Dad?" The thought was almost ridiculous. The feared paragon of industry, cooking outside over some well-arranged coals? Surely not!

Lewis also looked suitably proud of himself. "I certainly do," he said smugly. "Tasmin suggested it, so Tim and I went barbie shopping and bought home a bloody beauty." Coming from his father, the colloquial language was almost farcical, but Lachlan grinned widely. It was a wonderful sight to see his family so happy together, after the tensions of the past year.

If only he could capture Tasmin's attention and ease the awkwardness between them. He was resigned to her decision - he hated it, of course, and wished he could change her mind - but he knew his feelings had not and would not change. He accepted the fact he was in love with a woman who did not love him back. How the tables had turned. He almost felt guilty at the string of broken hearts he had carelessly left behind him. It did not seem so casual anymore, toying with someone's emotions.

"Sit with me, Uncle Lachy," Bethany exclaimed, shuffling excitedly in her seat. "Tassie and I have been colouring in." She held aloft the book of intricate designs for him to see. He dared a glance at Tasmin, but she did not meet his gaze. Lewis pulled out the timber chair beside Bethany and indicated he should sit. As soon as he did, Ava clambered into his lap.

"They are beautiful," he told Bethany, carefully appraising the colouring book, as if it was a work of a great artist. What a group they were, huddled here at one end of his parent's long kitchen table. Rosie was content spreading smashed banana across the tray of her highchair, and beside her sat Tasmin, then

Bethany, then he and Ava. It was cosy, wonderful, and agonising, all at once; Tasmin was close enough to reach out and caress, yet the distance between them was greater than ever.

The conversation rose around him as the adults filled their plates and discussed the comings and goings of the week. The tales wove around the room, and although Lachlan did his best to stay animated and involved, he felt almost removed from the rest of the family. Their happiness was evident, and he struggled to keep the envy from his heart. Even Tim, who had recently quietly admitted deep bouts of loneliness and dissatisfaction with his career, seemed back to his cheerful self, and Lachlan loved seeing the smile on Sara's face as she gazed tenderly at Rosie and her mess.

After a pleasant enough meal, a few hours of game show television and even more colouring in with the girls, Tim and Sara packed them into their four-wheel drive and headed home. Dawn gathered up Tasmin and Rosie, to ready them for the driver to collect, but before they left Tasmin handed the baby to him. It was the closest she had willingly come near him all evening.

"I think she has been missing you," she told Lachlan quietly.

"I miss her more than you know," he answered simply.

He wrapped her in his arms and breathed her in as Rosie relaxed against him, tired out from the constant stimulation of her older cousins, and kept her there, softly swaying his lean body until the driver arrived. When they left Lachlan stayed behind, absentmindedly clearing the table with Dawn before moving outside to admire Lewis' new barbecue, jibing his father as he conscientiously cleaned it down before closing the gleaming stainless-steel hood. He felt no rush to return to his work at the House or his empty penthouse, so he pottered behind his parents, brewing a pot of strong coffee for them all, and feeling more than a little pathetic. He really had no real friends he could turn to, so here he was, a grown man, hiding out in his parent's kitchen, trying to soothe a weary heart with caffeine.

As he sipped carefully at the steaming liquid, Lachlan noticed his parents, seated side-by-side at the counter, watching him. He raised his brows in question.

"What's wrong Lachlan?" It was Dawn who spoke first. "You are killing yourself at work, hiding out at Sara's or escaping into the hills with Tim. You avoid us, unless it's to speak to your father about the Foundation, and most of that you insist happens in your office, so we want to know what is going on with you."

Lachlan remained quiet, not because he did not want to answer but because he was not sure how to.

Dawn ploughed on. "I know you had that stupid incident at Tasmin's when Sara lost her temper, but I thought we were past all that." Lachlan stared at the patterns in the stone of the countertop, feeling both sets of eyes boring into him.

Lewis took over. "You are achieving a great deal right now Lachlan, and I am hearing good things from within the Party." Lewis always had his ear to the political ground; even before Lachlan's election he had been extremely well connected. "But none of that matters if something is troubling you."

"We've all noticed it," Dawn continued, upping the pressure a notch. "Even Marg is worried."

Lachlan took a shaky breath. What did he have to lose? *Only his dignity*, he thought. Look at him, hanging out here, confessing his feelings for a girl like an inept teenager. *Christ*, he cursed inwardly. In hindsight puberty had been a lot easier than this.

"I'm in love with her," he said simply, and both his parents sat back a little on their stools, mirroring each other's surprise. "I am in love with Tasmin, which is a fucking mess, and I told her, and of course she is not a frigging idiot, so she shut me down. Which is fine, I mean it makes perfect sense." He was babbling, even to his own ears Lachlan knew he sounded ridiculous.

Dawn cut in. "You're in love with Tasmin? Our Tasmin? Oh Lachy," she breathed out audibly. "That is a lot to take in." She looked to Lewis helplessly.

Lewis shrugged with a nonplussed air. "I knew that," he said, and both Lachlan and Dawn stared at him, speechlessly. "I've known that for some time. Probably before you realised yourself." He waved a hand at both of them. "Shut your mouths, you two.

You're both gaping like bloody guppy fish. It's been pretty darn obvious all along." He began to count off on his outstretched fingers.

"That's why Sara was so defensive; she thought she was losing her baby brother." Lewis put another finger down. "It's why you spent so much time trying to get Sara to accept Tasmin." Another finger went down. "It's why you are so besotted with Rosie; deep down you wish she was your child." Lewis calmly looked from mother to son. "And is it really so hard to accept? You have changed so much Lachlan. You are a truly wonderful man who deserves a truly wonderful woman. Not like those bits of fluff you paraded around in the past. Tasmin has substance, and a heart full of kindness, so of course you have fallen in love with her." Lewis placed an arm around his wife's shoulders and hugged Dawn to him. "She reminds me of you Dawn; so much beautiful potential." He kissed his wife on the forehead with gusto, before standing. "I am tired, and I am missing the late news, which I plan to watch in my bed in peace." He nodded at them both. "I shall leave you two to debate the rights and wrongs of all this, but I think it's bloody marvellous. Tasmin will see you for what you are, once she has healed herself, and then it will all work out in the end." With that, Lewis disappeared upstairs.

Neither Dawn nor Lachlan spoke for a moment. Instead, they watched Lewis's retreating back as he strode away, before turning back to face each other.

"What the fuck just happened?" Dawn said, and the uncharacteristic curse caused a short laugh to burst from Lachlan.

He leant forward and placed his forehead on the cool surface. "What the fuck indeed," he answered. Adult emotions were *hard.*

Head still down, Lachlan said, "Say something Dawn. Tell me what you think." He raised his head and looked at his mother. "Tell me what to do?"

Dawn did not answer straight away. She clasped her hands in front of her and licked her lips before she spoke. "I don't know that there is anything you can do," she said, and Lachlan groaned. Naively - stupidly! - he had hoped his mum could magically make all this better.

Dawn raised a hand. "Hear me out," she commanded. "You say you love Tasmin, and if that is true that is not something you can change." Lachlan nodded. He agreed; if he were able to change it perhaps he would, but unloving Tasmin was impossible.

"You also cannot force someone to love you if they don't." She spoke gently, but the truth stung painfully regardless. "Lewis is right - Tasmin is damaged, and maybe she will not ever be fully healed. She is distrustful, because she has had to be, and now she must also protect that baby." Dawn shook her head slightly as she spoke. "Of course, there is no chance of harm to Rosie, not from anyone, and certainly not from you, but logic won't change how Tasmin feels."

Dawn paused before taking another deep breath. "I need to share something with you Lachlan. A suspicion I vowed to keep to myself, but I think it may help you understand exactly what Tasmin is dealing with."

Another deep breath. Lachlan allowed her time to speak. The house was silent around them.

"I believe Logan hurt Tasmin. Really hurt her. I know he did, because Fairy told me as much, and I have seen some medical reports. Tasmin has told me a little, but never goes into much detail. I think she feels disloyal to me; she covers for me abandoning Logan." A tear slid down Dawn's cheek, and Lachlan placed a hand over Dawn's. "Logan was an addict, whose addiction and the lockdowns turned him into a dangerous and cruel man. I bear much of that responsibility and that guilt will never leave me." Lachlan ached at the anguish in Dawn's voice.

"The rest of my guilt is tied up with Logan's death," Dawn continued. "I had no plans to share this with anyone, even Lewis, but, well, here we are." She shrugged.

"Go on," Lachlan urged.

Another sharp intake of breath before Dawn rushed the words from her. "I think Tasmin and Fairy had something to do with Logan's death. I don't know how, but I can understand why. And that not only makes me a harsh person it makes me a wicked mother." A sob escaped and in an instant Lachlan had abandoned his coffee and raced to the other side of the island bench. He embraced Dawn, who laid her head on his chest and wept. When she regained control, Dawn pulled away, wiping her tears with her palms.

"I need to say this Lachy," she said. "I must. I believe Tasmin caused Logan's death to save her own life, and God forgive me I stand with her. The world went crazy, and you know what atrocities went unpunished during that mad time, but I turned Logan into a monster. I left him at the mercy of the system, and I failed him. He took his anger and rage out on an innocent girl, who did what she had to, to survive, and I cannot condemn her for that." The tears streamed down Dawn's face and Lachlan was having a hard time keeping up. He sat down on the stool left vacant by Lewis.

"You think Tasmin killed Logan? You think she *murdered* him?" The concept was unfathomable.

Dawn nodded. "God help me, I do," she said.

Blood pounded in Lachlan's head as he angrily drove around the city. He raced around corners and through red lights in the dark streets, trying to make sense of everything Dawn had shared with him.

Could she be right?

Was Tasmin capable of such an act?

Was she deliberately keeping a distance between them because of it?

Only one person could tell him the truth.

CHAPTER 18 - TASMIN

The pounding on her door startled Tasmin, who was standing wrapped in her thick robe in her bedroom, having just stepped from the shower. The thundering knocks sounded ominous and filled her with anxiety as she crept towards the door, but with relief she recognised Lachlan's voice.

"Tasmin it's me. It's Lachlan. Open the door. Tasmin?" All the while he knocked incessantly and Tasmin rushed to fling the heavy door of the apartment open. Now she felt a prick of annoyance at his arrogance.

"Shush!" she scolded as he swept past her into the living room. "Rosie is asleep, not to mention everyone else on this floor. You'll wake them all!"

When he turned towards her, Tasmin could see something was wrong. Lachlan held his shoulders so rigidly they seemed carved from stone, and his fists clenched and unclenched by his sides. He did not sit, choosing to stay upright meaning he dominated the space with his pent-up energy.

"I need to ask you one question." His tone was low, his words clipped.

Tasmin lay immobile and watched as the dark of the night faded and a dim, melancholy dawn slipped across the ceiling of her bedroom. She was prone on the wide bed, thankful for the rhythmic breaths of her sweet child beside her that provided a gentle background of snuffling white noise. She had not moved for hours, and her body felt like a dead weight. Dead. *Dead.*

The accusation was terrible, and yet the truth was so much worse. Tasmin feared she would never forget the look of absolute horror on Lachlan's face when she answered him. His eyes had widened and dulled at the same time, and he had searched her face as if to deny what she was telling him.

"Yes," she had answered, because what else could she have said? "I poisoned Logan with the virus, then drugged him until he died." The relief was incredible, as if a dark weight had been released like rotten smoke as she spoke the truth, but that reprieve was short lived. Lachlan had visibly recoiled, and the new weight of guilt and lost hope crashed down on her; she had just ruined all their lives.

He did not ask for details or excuses or reasons and she did not offer any. They stared at each other in deafening silence for what seemed like an eternity, until he abruptly turned and left. Then the tears had fallen.

She had wept for hours. She had tried to find the courage to call Dawn but could not. She tried to send a text message, yet that seemed even worse. Each thwarted attempt to salvage some of the family she had come to love pushed her further into a spiral of despair, until exhausted, the tears stopped, and she staggered to her bed.

Sleep would not come. Throughout the long hours her mind raced in a thousand different directions. Prison. Abandonment. Shame. Horror.

Rosie slept peacefully in the cot beside her and Tasmin knew when she woke, she would need to find the energy to gather her child and their few personal belongings and head to Fairy's home. They had nowhere else to go. The thought of moving an inch, of making any sort of decision, seemed impossible, and her own weakness brought fresh tears to her eyes. *I don't deserve any of them*, she thought. *Not Rosie, not the family or Fairy and most of all, I don't deserve Lachlan.*

Tasmin did not hear the phone ring. She was standing, motionless, as the scalding shower cascaded over her, stinging her skin, and blushing it pink with shame, the rush of water over her head doing nothing to drown out the memory of the shock in Lachlan's voice. When she slowly returned to her room and sat on the side of her bed, Rosie stared up at her, awake now in the early morning light, watching her mother. Tasmin felt her eyes fill with tears again. She had ruined Rosie's life. Her own life she cared little for, but in one conversation she had stripped her daughter of a family, a legacy, and a future.

Not in one conversation, she corrected herself. *In one, impetuous, necessary, evil act.* Her sin had been committed that fateful day when she took the jar from Fairy and took it inside that horror-filled home. The guilt she felt then had never really disappeared, but seeing it reflected in the dreadful disbelief in Lachlan's eyes tore the wound open, and a fresh pit of dread opened in her chest.

Who would raise Rosie when she was imprisoned? Fairy adored the child, but was an old woman, barely surviving herself, and Dawn would surely turn her back. Sara may take pity on a child, but Tasmin could only imagine Rosie being treated with icy disdain under Sara's watch, and images of a sorrowful, loveless childhood caused her to sob. Rosie startled and began to cry, so Tasmin scooped her into her arms and together they took refuge under the blankets.

On the bedside table beside her, her mobile phone chirped a message. Tasmin did not recall leaving it there but must have flung it aside last night after Lachlan left. She retrieved it and through red puffy eyes read the screen.

Three missed calls from Dawn. Tasmin switched the phone off, as panic rose in Tasmin's chest, and she shuddered. Leaving Rosie safely nestled into the pillows she dragged clothes onto a protesting body. Her limbs just wanted to lie down and not ever wake up, but Tasmin wanted to be clothed before the Police arrived to cart her away. She changed Rosie's nappy, fed her, and replaced her sleeping suit with a fresh one, before carefully restocking the nappy bag. As she placed Rosie's favourite toys and blanket inside, she strained to listen for a faint 'ping' that would herald the arrival of the lift to her floor. She wondered how many Police would arrive to arrest her.

When Rosie and she were dressed and ready, and both the baby's things and her own handbag were prepared Tasmin sat on the edge of the bed. She was confused. As anxious nausea rose in her throat Tasmin forced her hand to switch the phone back on, and immediately the screen lit up with notifications. Two more missed calls from Dawn and a text message.

"I know you have spoken to Lachlan. I want to explain. I have always known. I suspected, but I also knew. Please answer the phone."

With trembling fingers Tasmin shakily tapped out a message.

"I can't do this over the phone. Come here."

Dawn arrived in no time at all, and when Tasmin let her into the apartment she was surprised that Dawn was alone. The confusion must have shown, because Dawn gently said, "It's just me Tasmin. No one else." The pair sat opposite each other, both perched apprehensively on the edge of their armchairs, as Rosie quietly played on a rug between them. Tasmin felt as though he was watching the scene from outside of her own body, and the surreal nature of the moment made her feel slightly drunk with panic.

"I know Lachlan has spoken with you," Dawn began, speaking slowly and deliberately. "I spoke to him last night. He is shocked and uncertain and has no idea what to do next," Dawn paused momentarily, before crisply moving on. "He cares a great deal for you Tasmin, and we - he and I - have agreed that this goes no further."

Relief and confusion rushed through Tasmin's body, sending sparks of adrenaline to her fingertips.

"I... I don't understand," she stammered.

Dawn crossed the room and sat beside her. "Tasmin, I have always known something dreadful happened in that house." When Tasmin dropped her head to avoid Dawn's gaze, the older woman gently lifted her chin with one graceful finger. "Not Logan's death. That's not the dreadful part. I know he hurt you Tasmin. I have seen some of your medical reports, which should have been none of my business, but while we're all being honest here, I *have* seen them. And they ripped my heart apart. I can only imagine what your life was like..." Dawn paused, searching for the right words, "...before, but as a woman I can understand why you did what you did."

Tasmin could not believe what she was hearing. Dawn had always known?

"But," she stammered, then her voice dropped to a whisper. "I murdered your son."

Dawn leaned back in the chair as if suddenly overcome with fatigue. "Yes," she said simply. "It sounds like you did. But if you were to go to the

Police, Lewis would hire the best legal team this city has ever seen and you would be exonerated as a survivor of unspeakable abuse, so I - we - think it is best to just skip that step." She looked at Tasmin, unshed tears shining in her eyes. "For me, for Rosie, for our whole family, please say you agree with me." The sob escaped Tasmin, and she collapsed against Dawn, as sorrow and relief and gratitude erupted from her in a mess of mixed emotions. Dawn embraced the wailing girl, and gently rocked her until she calmed.

Once Tasmin had showered and pulled herself together the pair took Dawn's stately sedan out to the suburbs, with Rosie firmly strapped in the rear. When they pulled into Fairy's driveway Dawn strode across the porch and into the house to locate Fairy, leaving Tasmin to quickly remove Rosie from the car seat and hurry up the steps to join them.

When she burst into the kitchen, she could tell Dawn had delivered the news to Fairy, who was - for once - speechless. The spread of the truth that once only they had known, had robbed Fairy of her words.

"Say something," Tasmin implored. "Please Fairy, someone needs to tell me what to do next, and how to be after all this. It's too much." She slid into a hard backed kitchen chair, as her legs buckled under here. *God, she was so tired.*

Fairy straightened, then said. "Nothing to do next. Dawn is right. There is nothing to be gained from going to the coppers now, and baby Rosie needs you.

So. What's done is done, and that's the last of it."
Fairy looked over to Dawn, who nodded, and Fairy
added her own decisive nod of her head, her long grey
hair bouncing as she did so.

"I will get you some help Tasmin," Dawn added. "A
counsellor or someone you can confide in, who can
help you work through the guilt." She glanced across
to Fairy. "The *misplaced* guilt, you are feeling." Tasmin
looked at them both and was astonished to see
admiration on Fairy's face as she watched Dawn
speak. This was the most extraordinarily bizarre day.

CHAPTER 19 - LACHLAN

The interview wrapped up and Lachlan watched his father deliver the final few comments about the Foundation's work in the vaccination hubs and noted how he finished the interview. Lewis stared straight down the camera and spoke with steely determination. "It is my honour to lead the fight against this virus, and I know, together this country will get through this." Flashes popped as photographers eagerly captured the iconic image that Lachlan knew would grace front pages across the country in mere hours. He smiled ruefully to himself, with a mixture of pride and incredulity; Lewis truly was a seasoned player in this game of public relations and media manipulation. Together the pair had travelled the country for the past months, visiting countless hub co-ordination meetings with all tiers of Government officials, and Lachlan had witnessed Lewis in full organisational mode. Like a general at war, the older man had thrown all his negotiation skills, charm and resolve at getting clinics and training centres up and running, and his methods were working. Slowly at first, but then with surprising pace, the hubs were opening in town halls and disused schools around the nation, and the vaccination rate was skyrocketing. As the news of the successful model spread, Lewis was also spending precious hours – often in the middle of the night – discussing the concept with overseas Governments. Lachlan marvelled at his father's fortitude. The pace was maddening and would be draining for a person half Lewis' age, yet he seemed revitalised by the work and made gentle jibes at Lachlan's expense, whenever he lagged with exhaustion.

He endured his father's jokes with good humour, relishing the close bond the two had formed – for the first time in his life Lachan felt as if they were equals, and that his expertise and vast networks of contacts was vital to the whole operation. It was a new feeling for them both.

In truth, he also relished the exhaustion. The early mornings and late nights, the constant travel and endless conversations and problem solving meant he had little time to dwell on anything other than the vaccine roll out. He allowed little to enter his thoughts except work.

He deliberately steered his mind away from the way he had treated Tasmin, and how she might be feeling about him now.

In the first few days after Tasmin's revelation Lewis had attempted to discuss Logan's death with him, but Lachlan had quickly bought the conversation to an end. The last time the subject had been raised – no doubt at Dawn's insistence – Lachlan had simply risen from his place at the long-forgotten hotel bar and walked away. Lewis had not tried again.

As Lewis wound up a casual chat with some journalists he personally knew, Lachlan strode to his side. Lewis fell into step with him and together the powerful pair headed inside to where the real work would take place.

Lachlan wracked his brain to remember which small rural community they were visiting, and was grateful when a small, energetic middle-aged woman hurried towards them, her hand outstretched. "Welcome to Stanley Creek," she said, before quickly remembering pandemic protocol and withdrawing her hand. Lewis smiled at her gaffe and Lachlan was relieved she had answered his unspoken question.

"Sorry," she said, crestfallen. "Old habits, I suppose. This bloody virus has made everything so…" she raised her shoulders in a show of regret.

"…impersonal. I miss shaking someone's hand when I meet them. I even miss singing at the damn Christmas carols." She grinned at them both. "I bet no one else misses that though." Lachlan returned her smile. She reminded him of a younger, busier Fairy.

She motioned for them to follow her to where tables had been arranged in a square at one end of this hall. The community centre looked very much like the dozens Lachlan had visited recently. A small stage was curtained off at the opposite end with dusty faded velvet drapes, and along one long wall several serving windows opened through to what looked like a kitchen area. He could only imagine how many school concerts, weddings and debutante balls had been held here.

The small group assembled there turned expectantly as Lachlan and Lewis approached, their footsteps echoing on wooden floors, and the woman with them began rapid fire introductions.

"Mel Cook, Nurse Manager at the hospital, Bob Barker our mayor, Doug Gibson from the pharmacy and Stacey Johnson, our Police sergeant. Brady Kaur works with the employment agency group here in town and Norma Young is from the Aboriginal Medical Service." She looked around at the group, satisfied she had not missed anyone. "Of course, we all know who you both are. Thank you for coming." She gestured for everyone to take a seat, before looking expectantly at Lewis, then Lachlan, then back to Lewis. "I'll let you take it from here."

Lewis sat and nodded towards the woman. "Thank you so much, Ms... um?" His raised eyebrow asked the question.

"Oh!" The woman stammered and her cheeks coloured slightly. Lachlan imagined this was an important moment for her community and the oversight made in haste spoke volumes about her commitment to keeping it safe.

"Sorry jeeze, talk about forget my own head. I'm Rena Rossi. I'm the primary school principal and president of the Country Women's Association, Historical Society and Progress Association."

Lewis inclined his head in Rena's direction. "All important positions in Stanley Creek, I have no doubt. Thank you for bringing the group together."
Lachlan sat back and allowed his father's words to wash over him. He had heard all this before, many, many times, and he now preferred to watch the expressions on the faces before him, as Lewis outlined the strategy for vaccine rollout and the vital role community leaders had.
Lachlan's thoughts wandered as his tired mind thought back to the past weeks – no, months – on the road at his father's side. Together with a group of task orientated co-ordinators, eager Government representatives and serious medical experts, the father and son team had honed the processes involved with establishing vaccination hubs, and the training necessary to get unemployed people back to the front line of protecting their own towns and cities. The concept was working so well, thanks mainly to the local knowledge of dedicated focus groups such as the one before him today, that it was rapidly being replicated across the nation. The Foundation and Government relied on grassroots knowledge of people and their fears, to bring everyone through the doors, and currently in areas where hubs had been set up vaccination rates were among the highest in the world. The challenge now was to keep the momentum up and cover even the most remote corners of the nation. Lachlan calculated that their presence would soon become a mere publicity stunt, as the figureheads of

the Foundation, and the pair could return home for some down time. He had overheard his parents speaking just last night, as Lewis called Dawn to fill her in on the day's successes. Through thin country motel walls Lachan had heard his father's voice clearly, his pride obvious in every word.

"It's happening Dawn," he had said. "It's really working. Lachlan's idea will save this country and I am bloody proud to be at his side." He had paused and Lachlan had imagined his mother's loving response.

"That's right," Lewis had agreed, thousands of kilometres separating him from his wife. "Soon we will be able to come home and let the team take it from here. We'll just be needed for the ass kissing and interviews, which we can do from home. How soon? Oh, perhaps by the end of next week, I'd say. I know. It will be wonderful to get home."

Lachlan was not as eager to return to reality. The long hours and vast distances had been the ideal tonic to his guilt and inner turmoil, and he was not looking forward to ever facing Tasmin again.

His feelings were as confused and complicated as ever but time and distance had made on fact undeniable; he loved Tasmin, no matter what. But what did that even mean?

"We know crimes have been committed during lockdowns, and even beyond." It was the Nurse Manager speaking, and Lachlan tuned back into the conversation before him. "Women and children have lost their lives during this pandemic, and we know their deaths may never be treated as homicides." The woman spoke with passion, the words falling from her as she rushed to make herself understood. Lachlan could only wonder at the atrocities she had witnessed, in just this small town. What had she seen, that had made her reach out so desperately to his father? Mel Cook was leaning forward, her eyes locked on Lewis' as she continued to speak.

"Women and children have borne the brunt of this crisis, and until we can beat the virus and have our emergency services back doing their jobs protecting people instead of patrolling borders and processing permits, it will not end for victims of abuse. The death rate will continue to rise."

Beside her Norma Young placed a comforting hand on her shoulder. "Mel has been stretched beyond her role at the hospital," she explained. "But she has gone above and beyond to help too many women before it's too late." The woman's dark eyes swept the assembled group, pausing on the Police sergeant. "We all have, and sometimes we've been able to help. But in this town alone, seven women and two tiny children did not make it through lockdown."

Lachlan was shocked. "Seven? And children too?" He could not keep the dismay from his voice, and he wished he had paid more attention to the pleas of these mourning townspeople instead of daydreaming in the background. He glanced at Lewis, who seemed pale.

Norma and the others nodded solemnly. "Some are under investigation, and some have already been ruled accidental, which is a whole lot of bullshit, if you ask me." The Police sergeant opened her mouth as if to protest but the older woman held up a hand to silence her. "C'mon now Stacey, no need to cover for your superiors. No one around here is blaming you, b'cause we all know how hard you've been fighting too." She turned to face Lewis; her hands raised. "We need you Mr Wolfe. We need you to rid this town of the virus, so we can go back to looking after our own, before another tragic 'accident' gets swept aside b'cause it's not important enough right now."

Seargeant Johnson cleared her throat before speaking with careful authority. "It is true that several questionable deaths have occurred since the outbreak, and while I do not condone any efforts by Area Command to reclassify my officers, my hands have been tied. Are tied," she corrected. "The simple fact is we are a five officer station, and usually that works just fine, but during the pandemic cheap drugs and even bootleg grog streamed through this place and desperate frightened people took to them both." She looked at Lachlan and he could see the distress marring her face. "The results have been horrendous. Each day we wait with bated breath because behind closed doors anything could be happening."

"In normal times we see children every day at school," Rena chimed in. "We can often see when a family is becoming … overwhelmed, and we often step in to try to help avoid a crisis. When we see children every day we can keep an eye out for bruises, and we can make sure kids are eating and that they hear a kind word or two, but during lockdown all that disappeared overnight." Lachlan watched as unshed tears shone bright in the woman's eyes. "Education may have continued, via e-learning and bloody mail-out lessons, but that is only part of what we do." She too leant forward, using her body to make her point. "We are these kids safety net, and that disappeared at the very time they needed us most."

Lachlan was unable to offer any comment. How could he? Cocooned in the loving safety of his privileged family, he was ashamed of how he had spent lockdown. While people all over the world were in crisis – losing their lives even – he had enjoyed a secure career, a safe place to live and work, few financial stresses and had even been so arrogant as to engage in an affair with a married co-worker. The shame burned in his chest, and he excused himself, fleeing into the quiet, fresh air, leaving Lewis to handle the heart-breaking conversation.

Two weeks later Lachlan strode up the front path of Fairy's cottage but before he reached the verandah the door flung open and there stood Fairy herself, all intimidating five feet of her. Lachlan faltered a little at first but pushed himself forward.

"G'day," he said, and Fairy chuckled.

"Been out in the country, have we? You sound like a dickhead," she said but her smile was warm. "She isn't here, you know," she added. Lachlan did not need to ask what she meant.

"I know," he replied. "I've come for some advice."

Fairy raised one greying eyebrow and let out a low whistle. "You'd better come in then," she said holding open the screen door and ushering him into the kitchen.

She gestured to a seat. "I'll make the cuppas. You do the talking," she ordered, as she moved around the compact kitchen with practised ease.

Lachlan took a deep breath and jumped straight in. *No point being self-conscious now*, he figured. The words tumbled from him. He told the story sequentially explaining how he had realised his feelings for Tasmin, describing the night he told her of his love, and then Dawn's explosive revelation and his own shameful reaction. He was careful not to leave anything out; he was here for advice, not absolution, and sugar-coating his own words and actions would not help. He was sure Fairy would see through any half-truths anyway. By this time Fairy had placed a hot mug of dark sweet tea in front of him, dumping it heavily on the table in front of him, about the time he spoke of how he had berated Tasmin. She made no comment, but Lachlan was sure the surface of the kitchen table had taken the force of her displeasure with him.

Fairy sat across from him, listening silently until he ran out of words.

"Well," he said. "Am I wrong to want to see her? Is it unfair of me to want to see her?"

Fairy did not answer immediately. Instead, she sipped her tea, thoughtfully, until Lachlan thought he would lose his mind. *Don't speak,* he chided himself. Just wait. Patience was new territory for him. Hell, all this was new to him.

"I think," Fairy started, and Lachlan looked up to watch her speak. "I think you go to her, and you tell her everything you just told me." She sipped her tea, using it as punctuation. "You tell her you've been a sheltered asshole," *Sip.* "But that you've finally grown up." *Sip.* "Tell her how sorry you are. Ask her what you can do to make it up to her, and then you accept whatever she says." *Siiiiiiip.* "Because Lachy my love, this has fuck-all to do with you, and everything to do with whether Tasmin is ready for love. With you or anyone else. And ultimately, you will need to accept that."

Lachlan sighed and nodded, knowing she was right, and they sipped their tea in companionable silence. As he left, he thanked Fairy for her time, and was surprised when the older woman laughed aloud. "I'm not one of you constituents Senator," she scolded. "I'm a mate, someone you can call in and see whenever you like, so maybe don't go 'thanking me for my time'." Fairy waved her hands about and spoke the words deeply in a mock imitation of his own serious tone. It was Lachlan's turn to laugh, and for the first time in many months he felt much lighter.

"Thanks Fairy," he said, this time with genuine warmth. "I might just call in again soon."
Fairy nodded curtly, but her smile was now softer. At some stage during his visit she had defrosted a little. "Good,' she said. "I'd like that. I'd like it even more if you bought me some pods for that fancy coffee machine Dawn sent over. I can't buy them around here and those teabags taste like shit."

Lachlan drove home, and quickly changed before heading to the gym, on the second floor of his apartment building. Unlike past sessions he did not punish his body, ignoring the treadmill and weight benches in favour of a hot yoga class that had just started. Dubious at first, he soon relished the way his body responded to the unfamiliar positions. *Maybe this is what it feels like to not hate yourself so much*, he wondered, as the class drew to an end.
He slept soundly that night, for the first time in a long time.

Once the week ended and his Senate business and Foundation commitments were wrapped up to his usual high standard, Lachlan changed out of his suit and headed down the highway to Tim and Sara's country property. Sara knew he was on his way and had promised a full roast dinner to celebrate, declaring the girls were mad with excitement at his visit.
"I think Tim has missed you the most," she told him on the phone earlier in the week, when he rang to

make sure they would be home. "He's… I don't know what he is, but he isn't himself. One minute he's locked away in the study, and the next he's ignoring all his conference calls, which isn't proving popular with his Editor." Her sigh was audible, and Lachlan thought she sounded tired.

As he drove down their long dirt driveway to the house Lachlan felt his spirts lift as he spotted the house in the distance. The outside lights were ablaze and in the deepening dusk, with the setting sun as a backdrop, it looked like an oasis of tranquillity in the bush.

The front door burst open before he had even bought the car to a complete halt and Lachlan braced himself against the onslaught of his excited nieces. They tripped over themselves, their words spilling forth in their eagerness to capture his attention. He scooped them up in his arms, and grunted exaggeratedly at their weight, which caused shrieks of laughter.

The weekend passed in a haze of long lunches, late brunches and dinners prepared by them all in the large, homely kitchen. Tim declared it occasion enough to break out the good scotch and he and Lachlan wandered about the gardens and yards, talking a great deal about not much at all. Lachlan could feel the tension and stress of the past months ebb away like the early morning dew that steamed off the wide green lawns.

On Sunday afternoon Sara cornered him as he brewed a strong coffee to take with him on his journey back to the city.

"Has Tim said anything to you?" She did not bother with any small talk.

Lachlan was taken aback. "Huh?" he said. "He's said heaps, but what do you mean? Exactly?"

Sara rolled her eyes at him, an action that immediately threw him back to his seven-year-old self, trying to impress his confident older sibling.

"I told you," she said, the exasperation clear in her voice. "He just isn't himself. I was hoping he would open up to you at some stage over the weekend." She sat heavily on a kitchen stool, placed her elbows on the bench and lay her head in her hands. "It's mainly why I agreed to you coming up this weekend. I was hoping to get some answers."

"Gee thanks," Lachlan said dryly. "I thought you were just happy to see me."

Again, Sara rolled her eyes at him, this time deliberately. "I am. You know I am. I was just hoping …" Her voice trailed off and she replaced the words with a small shrug of her shoulders.

Lachlan poured hot coffee into his travel mug, breathing in the rich aroma. "Tim and I have just enjoyed a relaxing weekend, talking about nothing heavy at all, which is probably just what we both needed. I know I did."

Sara made a noise, somewhere between a snort and a laugh. It was a harsh sound, almost unkind.

Lachlan raised his eyebrows. "What?"

Sara sighed again. "What do you have to be stressed about Lachy? You are the apple of the nation's eye right now, Lewis's pride and joy and 'our country's saviour'." She used her fingers to provide air quotes for the last phrase, taken from the latest headline about the Foundation's work. Lachlan was hurt but busied himself stirring sugar into the dark liquid, so the sting of Sara's jealousy was not obvious to her. He took a deep breath. "There is something I wanted to talk to you about." With that Lachlan poured out the whole story of the preceding month. He had not expected to be having this conversation with Sara – he was not even sure it was any of her business – but the opportunity had arisen, so he took it. He told her everything; his feelings for Tasmin, her reaction, his angry words, the dreadful reality of life during lockdown and his visit to Fairy. He left out any mention of Logan's death; that was not anything anyone else needed to know.

As he ran out of words, he finally faced Sara squarely. "Your turn," he said. "Say something."

Sara's voice was low, and her words deliberate and slow.

"Of course. Of-bloody-course. The entire family is madly in love with this... this... *trespasser*, so of course the Playboy Senator just has to have himself a piece." She slid from the chair and stood in front of him.

"I'll just wait," she said bitterly. "You chew women up and spit them out like used gum Lachy, so this thing –

whatever it is – with Tasmin won't even be an issue in a few weeks. I'll just wait till then."

Lachlan was stunned at her words. "I've seen you with Tasmin," he cried. "I've seen you warm to Rosie, how you love, even if you refuse to admit it. Why the hell are you determined to be so fucking cruel to me?"

Sara shook her head dismissively. "Get along Lach. You don't want to be travelling in the dark and honestly I don't think there is much else I want to hear from you right now."

From the hall doorway Tim spoke firmly. "Cut it out Sara, before you say something you really regret."

The siblings started; neither of them had heard him arrive. Sara opened her mouth to speak, but Tim's presence fortified Lachlan. He picked up the mug from the bench and slid his phone into his back pocket before turning to face his sister.

"I don't know what has gotten into you, but you DON'T get to treat me like a child anymore Sar. I have lived my entire life in your golden girl shadow and now – finally – when I have come to my sense and begun to take my life and my career and my future seriously, you want to dismiss everything I do and everyone I care about." Lachlan looked at her with fresh eyes, not liking the way her anger thinned her lips as she bit back a harsh retort.

"I have had a wonderful few days with you all, so I am going to choose to forget this little tantrum of yours but hear me now. I don't know what will happen with Tasmin and I, but I will not ever allow you to make

her feel anything other than a loved and respected part of this family." He pointed at Sara to emphasis his point. "Either accept Tasmin and Rosie or stay out of my way. I am more than happy to hang out with Tim and the girls without you."
Lachlan strode from the room, stopping only to give Tim a resounding high-five clap as he marched down the long hallway and out into the late afternoon.

CHAPTER 20 - TASMIN

Tasmin looked down at Rosie babbling away in the pram, waving her chubby arms in the midday sunshine, as the crossed the parkland towards their home. The day had been so warm and inviting that Tasmin had escaped the apartment as soon as they had both finished their breakfast. Pushing Rosie, she had wandered the inner-city suburbs for hours, stopping to enjoy a coffee at an outdoor café and admiring lush gardens as they strolled. She chatted to people she passed and bought a bunch of fresh flowers from a vendor near the train station. Despite her initial reservations she loved this suburb now and had even become friendly with other parents she ran into at the park.

Heading the pram towards their home, Tasmin walked slowly, enjoying the languid pace in the spring warmth. As she neared their apartment, she noticed a familiar figure seated on the low stone wall that separated the apartment forecourt from the footpath. Lachlan. Unbidden, her heat skipped a beat and her skin flushed with heat.

He looked more handsome than she remembered. She
had spent many hours remembering the look of
disgust on his face as she admitted her part in Logan's
death but had steadfastly decided to put him from her
mind, as a coping mechanism. He had declared his
love for her once, which was incredible enough, but
now, burdened by the entire truth, she expected to
never see him again. With massive effort, she had
cleared her mind of any thought of him.

Yet here he was, darkly gorgeous, and apparently
waiting for her. She approached him but had no
words, instead coming to a silent halt a couple of steps
away from him.

"Looks like we both had the same idea," he said,
gesturing to the modest bunch of flowers balanced
atop Rosie's pram. In his arms he held an enormous
array of blooms, tiny blue wildflowers, scented
eucalypt branches and rich red waratahs.

"Seems we did," her voice wavered noticeably, and she
cleared her throat, before straightening her shoulders
as if to muster some unseen sense of strength. "What
are you doing here Lachlan?"

"I have come to apologise," he said simply. "The
flowers are probably overkill, but Dawn said bring
them anyway." His effortless shrug was charming.

"Dawn?" Tasmin hated that she seemed incapable of
full sentences.

"Yes, Dawn," he answered. "Dawn knows I am here,
to offer whatever sort of apology is necessary to make
up for how I last left you. I am here to tell you how

stupid I've been and – as Fairy suggested – offer to do whatever it takes to make it up to you."

"Fairy?" *God, will I ever speak properly again*, Tasmin wondered.

Lachlan nodded. "Tasmin I am so, so sorry at how I have treated you. I am so out of my depth right now, having never felt this way about anyone before."

Tasmin's heart thudded almost painfully in her chest.

"I needed to ask the wise women in our life how to fix this." His eyes pleaded at hers. "I'm sorry if that has upset you, but I needed to know how to approach you without making it worse." He laughed. "In the end it was Lewis who gave the best advice." Tasmin cocked her head at him, not daring to speak.

"My father said, 'For Christ's sake Lachlan just go and see Tasmin, tell you how atrociously you've acted and beg her forgiveness.'"

Again, he shrugged gracefully, taking a deep breath before saying, "So here I am, begging your forgiveness." He watched her intently and waited for her to speak.

Tasmin took a moment, looking from Lachlan to Rosie who was gurgling and smiling up at Lachlan like a long-lost friend.

"Why does it matter?" she asked. "Why do you even need my forgiveness? I am the one who has an act to be forgiven, no one else."

Lachlan shook his head, and without disclosing those dreadful details, he explained to her all he had learned on this trip with Lewis.

"I understand," he said simply. "I may not have before, because the truth of lockdown and abuse and violence is so foreign to me, but after hearing those stories, I can only imagine the decision you were faced with." He crouched down beside the pram and took Rosie's tiny pale hand in his own. "Imagine if you hadn't been so strong," he whispered.

Tasmin felt emotion rush through her body and her throat ached with unshed tears, but she fought for composure as Lachlan continued.

"I told you once that I loved you Tasmin," he was not looking at her, instead he stayed crouched, his gaze on Rosie. "That hasn't changed. I love you but I now better understand why you turned me away." He looked up at her and Tasmin was surprised to see he too was fighting back tears.

"I will never hurt you Tasmin. You or Rosie. I am in love with you, but I will wait until you are ready for that. And if you are not ever ready, well, I'll just have to deal with that too." He rose, towering over her, but mindful to keep a respectful distance between them.

"I love you, I will wait for you, and I am sorry. That's what I came here to say."

Overruling her brain Tasmin's heart forced her to step forward, closing the short space between them. Who cares, she thought. Who cares about the past? Who cares about the future? This is here and now and this is what I want.

She raised her hand and placed a cool palm on his cheek. It felt flushed, and the short stubble of his face rasped against her skin. She answered him, not with words, but with a soft kiss.

Lachlan stood still for a moment, but as his brain caught up and he realised what had happened, he wrapped an arm around her slight waist and pulled her close. They kissed deeply, one arm on each other and the over interlaced protectively on the handle of the pram.

Behind them, in the busying street a car horn tooted appreciatively, and the couple drew apart to smile shyly at each other.

CHAPTER 21 - THE WOLFE FAMILY

Lachlan looked across the garden to where Dawn, Fairy and Tasmin sat, chatting, and watching Rosie as she raced by on a new trike, her fourth birthday present. The garden was filled with children and their parents, friends of Rosie's from kindergarten, and some close Party associates. Bethany, now a pre-teen, was much too cool for kid's parties, and was snuggled up on the love seat, scrolling endlessly through her phone, but Ava was noisily chasing Rosie around as she rode.

Fairy looked old and tired, but refused any home help from anyone, while Dawn looked as unlined and refined as ever, refusing to grow old gracefully; regular trips to the plastic surgeon were now back on her agenda.

Lachlan passed his father a glass of freshly squeezed juice and Lewis murmured his thanks.

"The garden looks wonderful," he commented, between sips.

Lachlan laughed. "None of my doing," he said, as he looked around the walled grounds.

Never in a million years had he ever imagined living in a home like this. For a couple of years, he and Tasmin had slowly built their relationship, bumping their insecurities and quirks together until they married, more than a year ago. Until then they had not shared a home; spending time at each apartment, but as time passed the sleek penthouse had lost all its appeal to Lachlan.

In the month's leading up to their wedding he had taken Tasmin to every open house within commuting distance of the House, but it was she who had found this place. On one of her walks around the neighbourhood of her apartment, she stopped to chat to an elderly couple, who mentioned they were looking to downsize. A few enquiries and a couple of inspections later Tasmin had fallen in love.

The home was two storeys, built at the turn of the century of red brick with iron balustrades. The rooms were large and the ornate ceilings high, but it had needed a lot of repair. Their unlikely ally was Sara, who used all her contacts and force of will to have the renovations completed in record time, and Lachlan had carried his bride over the threshold of their new home.

Looking around the small crowd Lachlan marvelled at how much had changed. Tasmin glowed with the beauty of her second pregnancy, a boy due in just six weeks. Sara looked lonely and fragile, and Lachlan's heart broke anew for his sister, but he knew the only way forward for her was forward, with them all at her side. His parents and Fairy were in reasonable health, given their ages and Rosie was a constant delight. His nieces were blossoming into young women, although Beth was showing to be a stronger willed challenge than Sara had ever been.

The virus had all but been eliminated and the last death had been more than 12 months ago, a milestone the nation celebrated.

Lachlan looked down at Lewis, where he sat, before reaching down and giving his father's thin shoulder a gentle squeeze.

"I think we are all going to be alright," he said.

"Of course we are," Lewis said. "I always knew we would be."